The Man Nobody Can Ignore

Joseph DeGraft-Amanfu

Copyright © 2010 Joseph DeGraft Amanfu

All rights reserved. No part of this publication may be reproduced in any manner without written permission in advance, except in the case of brief quotations embodied in articles and reviews.

ISBN 978-1-60725-819-3

*All quotations are from the King James Version unless stated otherwise.

In this book, the term 'man,' represents male and female in most cases.

Also by Joseph DeGraft-Amanfu:

Second Chance ISBN 978-1-6064352-6-7
Transcended Life (paperback) ISBN 978-1-60643-527-4
Transcended Life (hardcover) ISBN 978-1-60725-820-9

Dedication

I dedicate this great book to all who desire to know the truth about Jesus Christ, the Son of the living God, who is gone into heaven, and is on the right hand of God with the angels, authorities, and powers being made subject unto him.

Further, it is dedicated to all who seek a better and purer life here and hereafter, and to them, who by patient continuance in well-doing, seek glory, honor, immortality, and eternal life.

Finally, I dedicate this book as a Bible study aid for pastors and Christian workers: "That the man of God may be perfect thoroughly finished unto all good works," Amen.

Acknowledgment

To Chief Editor Stephen Bess, and Editor Jan Montoya, I say many thanks for your valuable contribution, time and editorial work. May you be blessed with long life, peace and prosperity.

Also, special thanks to my precious wife, Miranda. You will always be my beloved wife.

Last, but not the least, my gratitude goes to all who are standing in prayer with me; you are indeed my pillar of strength. May the Lord open unto you all His good treasure, and bless all the work of your hands.

To get the most out of this book, please read this book alongside the Bible.

Table of Contents

Introduction ix
Prayer Request xvii
Chapter 1: The Revealed Will of God 1
Chapter 2: The God of the Bible 7
Chapter 3: Dateless Past 17
Chapter 4: Why God Became a Man 29
Chapter 5: Jesus Christ and Creation 49
Chapter 6: The Seed of the Woman 55
Chapter 7: The Seed of Abraham 79
Chapter 8: The Seed of David 85
Chapter 9: The Son of Man 89
Chapter 10: Jesus and the Holy Spirit 99
Chapter 11: The Son of God 107
Chapter 12: He Spoke with Authority 123
Chapter 13: His Own Claims 129
Chapter 14: His Teachings 141
Chapter 15: His Works 151
Chapter 16: Christ and His Church 159
Chapter 17: What Must I Do? 179
Chapter 18: Behold the Man 191
The Epitome of Christian Truth 197
About the Author 199

INTRODUCTION

I am pleased you have chosen to read this book. This is no ordinary book. I pray you approach it prayerfully and not with a blank mind, but with an open mind and heart. At the end of your reading you would know if you have already made the most important decision in life and if not, be able to ultimately make one.

There is a consciousness of God within every human soul. All people have some innate awareness of God. That which may be known of God is manifest in every human being without exception (Romans 1:19). The signature of the moral governor of the universe is on all that He has made such as man and nature.

Every human being has a mind; it is a gift from God. From the moment of birth to the end of physical life, all that is learned, heard, and observed are recorded in the mind. Innate knowledge and that which is learned, constitutes our thought processes. Words are simply the expression of thoughts and those thoughts determine our actions.

The content of our mind differentiates us from each other. It is what makes us different from one another. Social classifications, economic advantage, illustrious ancestry and other physical heredities may contribute little to who a person truly is, but the mind is who we are.

Religiously, every man is what he is in the mind and heart: "For out of the abundance of the heart the mouth speaketh." The human heart, which is the seat of emotions, feelings, intellect and morality must be kept with all diligence for out of it are the issues of life (Proverbs 4:23). The truth of God's law is written in every human heart.

What comes out of the heart through the mouth is that which defiles or makes a person unclean (Mathew 12:34; cf. 15:11). What each of us will become in this life and hereafter can be determined by what governs the mind and heart. "Life is enriched or impoverished, blessed or cursed, dignified or degraded by the ideas that govern our heart and mind."

Again, what we believe influences our decisions and governs our actions. A heart that is full of faith in the one and only true God is life. A correct knowledge of God leads to a correct view of God. Faith, which comes from God's word, is man's most precious gift. Faith in God has great recompense of eternal blessing. It draws the power of God for personal benefit and primarily for His glory (Jeremiah 17:5-13; Romans 8:6).

There is also a conscience in every human being, which is a free gift from God. We can all come to some conclusions of the existence of a moral governor through the conscience. Even though it does not give us power to be saved, it provides us with a sense of right and wrong.

Every man can know God for He has so ordered the affairs of every man in such a way that we can seek and find Him; therefore, man is without excuse (Romans 1:20). Even though the image and likeness of God upon man is corrupted because of sin, it is still recognizable in so many ways (cf. Genesis 1:27):

"That they should seek the Lord, if haply they might feel after him, and find him, though he be not far from every one of us:

For in him we live, and move, and have our being" (Acts 17:27-28).

Nature is another gateway to the knowledge of God or the existence of the Supreme Being. Physical nature displays a natural revelation of God. The power and wisdom of God is revealed through nature.

Though nature cannot tell us about sin or the salvation through Jesus Christ, we can all come to some conclusions of the existence of the Creator or the Supreme Being:

Introduction

"The heavens declare the glory of God; and the firmament showeth his handiwork" (Psalm 19:1).

Finally, and most importantly, God has revealed Himself to man through His only Son, Jesus Christ. Jesus Christ is the true representation of the invisible God. The invisible God is made visible in the person of Jesus Christ. Jesus Christ is the "express image of His person" (Hebrews 1:3). Jesus said:

"He that hath seen me hath seen the Father" (John 14:9).

Jesus Christ is the Gospel or the Good News. He came that we may have a Gospel to preach. Through the Gospel, man can be reconciled to the Creator who is not far from any of us. There is a chord in every man that still vibrates to the truth of God's word. Many times, ignorance of God is due to moral short-coming rather than to any mental difficulty. Knowledge of the truth is freedom and life (cf. John 8:32).

Honestly, there is very little information about historical Jesus Christ outside the Bible; even then, most of it is unlikely to be authentic. Amidst the volumes of books written, only the Bible can give a full and final revelation of the man whom it claims to be fully man and fully God.

The Bible is the only book that stands out as an authority and authentic testimony of the historical Son of God. Not only is Jesus Christ the crux of the bible, but He is also its supreme subject, especially, the New Testament.

In Him, the Old Testament makes a lot of sense – it becomes complete and purposeful. The Old Testament ceremonies, laws and prophecies find their fulfillment in Him. The many rivers of the Old Testament prophecies become one main river of fulfillment in the person of Jesus Christ in the New Testament.

Through Jesus Christ, every man can truly know the one and only true God. Where we individually stand in our belief concerning Jesus Christ, the Savior-Messiah is essential to our very existence. God presents His Son to the entire world as the one in whom He delights.

The most powerful and influential man in history and in the universe is not subject to any man's scrutiny. God did not send His Son into the world to be vetted by mankind. Being self-existing and self-sustaining, Jesus does not need any man's endorsement or approval.

God is satisfied with the impeccable character and vicarious expiatory mission of His dear Son and has crowned Him Lord of all:

> **"Here is my servant, whom I uphold, my chosen one in whom I delight; I will put my Spirit on him and he will bring justice to the nations"** (Isaiah 42:1; cf. Mathew 17:5; Luke 3:22).

Even though, Jesus Christ message is, in many ways, a stumbling block and a rock of offense to the Jew, and foolishness to the non-Jew, He is God's only answer to the human cry (1 Corinthians 1:23). No man can be saved from sin, death, and the wrath of God except through Him. That which is impossible with men is possible through Jesus Christ.

The world has witnessed many great and noble men – men of statue and of great ideas, men who ranked among the best. They all may have been known for ethical purity and even considered as Messiah's, demi-gods or saviors; however, of all who were born into this world, only Jesus Christ has claimed to be God and substantiated his claim by his lifestyle, powerful words, miracles, death, resurrection, and ascension.

People who saw and heard Jesus Christ wondered what manner of man He was. They did not see a mere man, but a man who spoke like God and did the works only God can do:

> **"And they feared exceedingly, and said one to another, what manner of man is this, that even the wind and the sea obey him?"** (Mark 4:41).

For the last two thousand years, people of all nations, tribes, and cultures have been blessed through the power of His name. Many people afflicted with divers sicknesses and diseases are being set free even at this moment. Satan and his fallen angels of demons tremble at the mere mention of the name of Jesus Christ.

Both History and the Holy Bible bear witness that historical Jesus Christ stands alone and above men of every generation. No man has gathered around his claims and characters such voluminous literature as Jesus Christ. He is the only man in history that has more books written, more words spoken, and more opinion uttered about Him, and no man even comes close.

Further, no single individual since the beginning of the world has gathered behind him more followers than Jesus Christ. Today, more than one-third of the world's populations are His followers. Here is an eye witness account – someone who saw, handled and ate with Him:

"This is the disciple which testifieth of these things, and wrote these things: and we know that his testimony is true.

And there are also many other things which Jesus did, the which, if they should be written every one, I suppose that even the world itself could not contain the books that should be written. Amen" (John 21:24-25).

Technically, Jesus the Christ is the official name of God who became man. As to the significance of His double name: 'Jesus' is the Greek form of the Hebrew 'Joshua' which means 'Yahweh saves.' Being a common name, Jesus is generally distinguished from other bearers of the same name by the addition of 'Nazareth.' Sometimes, when the life of Jesus is in reference, the name 'Jesus,' alone is usually used.

The second name, "Christ or Messiah," means "the Anointed One" or the "Anointed of God." This second name, "Christ or Messiah," differentiates Him from all other men bearing the name Jesus. Jesus Christ is the expected Hebrew Messiah. The Bible is clear on the significance of His name:

> "And she shall bring forth a son, and thou shall call his name JESUS: for he shall save his people from their sins" (Mathew 1:21)

There are other names ascribed to Him that shall be considered throughout this book. To be rightly informed means you are responsible to make the right decisions. God is absolute truth and truth has the inherent power to set every man free from all errors. Heresy is the denial of revealed truth.

This timely book will expose you to the truth of God's God. That man broke the one and only law given to humanity by representative man Adam and his wife Eve, is fully revealed in the Bible. Because of the fall, there is an indictment against the whole world because all men are under sin. Further, because all have sinned, Jesus Christ has become the standard from whom all men shall be judged at the end of the ages.

The good news is that the Gospel of Jesus Christ can save all who come to God pleading for mercy and grace, and there is no difference. Any man who places his faith in Jesus Christ and accepts Him as Lord and Savior shall be saved. The Gospel of Christ is the power of God unto salvation to every man that believeth (cf. Romans 1:16).

Jesus Christ represents all that is new and pleasing to God. He is the representative New man – He represents all who are born anew or the new people of God (2 Corinthians 5:17). The will and pleasure of God is that every man would be conformed into the image and likeness of His Son (Romans 8:29; 1 John 3:2).

The Bible is clear that one day every knee in heaven, on earth, and under the earth shall bow at the mention of the name of Jesus Christ and that every tongue shall confess that Jesus Christ is Lord to the glory of God the Father (Philippians 2:10-11). God commands every man to listen to Him.

Today, the world is ruled by ideals and the ideas of men. Ideas are the deciding factors in our highly industrialized, technological, scientific, and information age. However, none of us can argue against the fact that many of the evolving ideas seem to threaten our very existence.

More than ever, people in the world are questioning the deity and manhood of Jesus Christ. Even, in the theological arena there are debates as to whether Jesus the Christ is truly God or a mere man with supernatural capabilities. It appears Jesus Christ is being squeezed between many faiths.

For some, the purpose is to discredit Him; however, many are genuine in their search to know the truth about historical Jesus Christ. The idea that there are many roads to salvation and possibly to heaven is being taught in both religious and secular institutions. Example of such is pluralism – the belief that there is more than one way to God or to heaven.

Honestly, there is nothing wrong with having great and noble ideas. But the rule is that, they must be the right ideas. The word of God is the purest and the highest of ideals for mankind (Psalm 119:160). No nation or individual can survive or live up to its highest dreams outside the moral standard of the Bible.

The goal of this book is to give you the rarest opportunity to take a second look at the man who claims to be the only Son of God. This book presents historical Jesus Christ from God's point of view and as recorded in the holy Bible.

It is about time we face the examination of our own conscience in respect to the only man in the history of humanity that claims to be fully God and fully man. After all, we can only accept or reject Him for who He claims to be. Truth cannot be destroyed or changed, all we can do is to reject or accept it.

If the eternal well-being of every human soul is intrinsically bound to Jesus Christ, then it is essential that the truth is presented in a manner that would enable every human being to make the right decision. This is the goal of this book.

Personally, I do not believe it is too late for any human being or man to re-educate the mind concerning the truth. No man is beyond the grace of God. The Word of God is able to recreate the mind and provide every man with a new heart and a new spirit:

> "For the word of God is quick, and powerful, and sharper than any twoedged sword, piercing even to the dividing asunder of soul and spirit, and of the joints and marrow, and is a discerner of the thoughts and intents of the heart.
>
> Neither is there any creature that is not manifest in his sight: but all things are naked and opened unto the eyes of him with whom we have to do" (Hebrews 4:12-13).

Admittedly, to be led by the Spirit of God to write a book on the only Son of God is no mean task. It is purely by the grace and sovereignty of God that I have been chosen to add to the few books on the shelf about Him.

Further, I do not in any way consider this work as my own achievement and neither do I deserve any credit for its contents. I am intensely thankful to my Lord, teacher, instructor, and companion the Holy Spirit, who not only honored me with such an eternal blessing by electing me, but literally guided my thoughts throughout the writing of this book.

My only prayer is that you do not judge this book by its grammar, simplicity, or modest style of presentation. I am only a servant in the service of my master. All credit must be given to God.

PRAYER REQUEST

"I exhort therefore, that, first of all, supplications, prayers, intercessions, and giving of thanks, be made for all men. For kings, and for all that are in authority; that we may lead a quiet and peaceable life in all godliness and honesty.

For this is good and acceptable in the sight of God our Saviour; who will have all men to be saved, and to come unto the knowledge of the truth.

For there is one God, and one mediator between God and men, the man Christ Jesus; who gave himself a ransom for all, to be testified in due time" (1 Timothy 2:1-6).

Chapter 1

THE REVEALED WILL OF GOD

It may be a surprise to you that this book begins its first chapter with such a title. If it is, then accept my apology. Here is my reason: it is expedient to begin this way because almost all of what we know about Jesus Christ comes from the Bible, especially the New Testament. Jesus Christ is an enigma unless one accepts the record of the Bible.

Another reason is that this book relies 100% on the testimony of the Bible, especially that of the Gospels Mathew, Mark, Luke, and John. The Bible is the revealed will of God. In it, the will and ways of God towards man are clearly presented. They are simple, logical, and unsophisticated.

Honestly, if the Bible is not the word of God in its entirety, then man is in deep trouble, but to God be the glory it is. It is comforting to the human heart that man does not have to comb the entire universe or search under every tree and brush for the right God and Savior:

"The testimony of the Lord is sure, making wise the simple (Psalm 19:7).

The Bible is the word of the living God. Unlike any other book or literature, the Bible is "inspired." This means every word in the Bible is God-breathed:

"All scripture is given by inspiration of God, and is profitable for doctrine, for reproof, for correction, for instruction in righteousness: That the man of God may be perfect, thoroughly furnished unto all good works" (2 Timothy 3:16-17).

God is truth and so is every word from His mouth. Apart from the Bible being the word of God, which of course sets it apart from any other book or literature, the men who were chosen to write it wrote as if God was personally writing.

Further, these men wrote as though they were in control and free to choose their own style of presentation. God the Holy Spirit spoke and directed the writers the very things to say and write. Of all the books ever written, the Bible is the most wonderful in its meaning, and message.

The contents of the Bible are everlasting in truth, infallible and ethically incomparable:

"All Scripture is given by inspiration of God, and is profitable for doctrine, reproof, for correction, for instruction in righteousness: That the man of God may be perfect, thoroughly furnished unto all good works" (2 Timothy 3:16-17; cf. Job 32:8).

God purposefully gave the Bible to make His will and purpose known to man. He gave to mankind one book to guide men of every generation – the same and one book as the light to light the path of every man that is born into the world. Superficially, every generation may be different, but fundamentally are the same. The Bible is a one-book solution for all time human needs. At the heart of all human problems is the problem of the human heart.

Further, God did not give to man an open-ended book. The Bible is complete and sealed (this does not mean God is not revealing more of Himself through the written word). No man can add or take from it (Revelations 22:19-19). It has a promise of blessing for all who choose to heed the warning and obey its contents:

> "For I testify unto every man that heareth the words of the prophecy of this book, If any man shall add unto these things, God shall add unto him the plagues that are written in this book.
>
> And if any man shall take away from the words of the book of this prophecy, God shall take away his part out of the book of life, and out of the holy city, and from the things which are written in this book" (Revelations 22:18-19).

Further still, the Bible is not given to humanity for the sole purpose of explaining the person of God. The Bible assumes the existence of God. It has as its subject, the Lord Jesus Christ, and its object the salvation of man, and its consummation the eternal reign of Christ.

The Bible became a necessity because of the event of the fall of man (Genesis 2). God gave the Bible to testify of His hatred for sin and His remedy for sin through His appointed Savior and redeemer. It speaks of what God has done for the human race through His only Son whom He had appointed Savior and Lord.

Again, the Bible is a love letter from the Creator to His fallen and estranged children – the human race. It reveals that God is in Christ, "reconciling the world unto himself" (2 Corinthians 5:19). The Bible reveals Jesus Christ as the love of God personified and expressed. God the Father sacrificing His Son is Love's last word:

> "Herein is love, not that we loved God, but that he loved us, and sent his Son to be the propitiation for our sins" (1 John 4:10; cf. John 3:16).

The Biblical injunction to "love one another," is based on the fact that, "God laid down His life for us" (1 John 3:16). And we know that it is "Jesus Christ" who laid down His life for us:

> "Hereby perceive we the love of God, because he laid down his life for us: and we ought to lay down our lives for the brethren" (1 John 3:16).

The Bible is divided into two main books: The Old Testament which tells about the preparation of the coming of the Savior-Messiah or King, and the New Testament which testifies to the fact that the Savior-Messiah has come and fulfilled all prophecies and is coming the second time to earth to set up an everlasting Kingdom of peace and righteousness. Without the New Testament the Old Testament is far from being complete.

The Bible as the revealed will of God places great demand on every human being to re-examine life through its contents (cf. Ecclesiastes 12:13). As God's word, the Bible is not subject to any man's private interpretation.

Because it is sealed, only the Spirit of God can unlock its meaning to the thirsty and searching heart. It may be a closed book to some people, especially to the unbeliever, but it is an open book for all who hunger and thirst after the truth and righteousness.

Honestly, I do share the concerns of those who believe that God is more than what the Bible reveals, but this is what I have to say to them, since the Bible is the only authentic record from the hands of the Creator, it is wise for each of us to be content with it. I do not think man has any choice in this matter:

> "**Knowing this first, that no prophesy of the Scripture is of any private interpretation. For the prophesy came not in the old time by the will of man: But holy men of God spake as they were moved by Holy Ghost**" (2 Peter 1:20-21).

Believe it or not, any alternative is nothing short of man's continuous rebellion against the will of God. Many of the religious books on our bookstore shelves and libraries today, and I say this with respect, are not factual. Instead, they are strange doctrines which are hard to explain and impossible to arrive at any logic.

They provide no illumination, but are like the blind leading the blind. They carry no truth and no power to emancipate man from sin or give new life to those who hope in them. The Bible is sufficient; therefore, it must be accepted by all. Anything new and in contra-distinction to the written word, should be utterly rejected and regarded as heresy; it does not matter how sound or rational they may appear to be. Here is my plea and counsel:

> "If it is not in the Bible, it is not worth knowing. Amen"

Besides, since every man shall sooner or later appear before God the Creator, we should be content to reserve whatever questions or concerns to that day. Let each man pay heed to this admonishing:

> "The secret things belongs unto the Lord our God: but those things which are revealed belong unto us and to our children forever, that we may do all the words of this law" (Deuteronomy 29:29).

False doctrine and false religion is cancer to the soul; therefore, I pray every man to be content with the truth as revealed in the Bible. The word of God, in many ways, may transcend our reasoning, even beyond the reach of any human investigation, but we can fully understand and accept them as truths to live by if we depend on the Holy Spirit:

> "But there is a spirit in man: and the inspiration of the Almighty giveth them understanding" (Job 32:8; 33:4).

The only one and true God of the universe is knowable, but not through self-effort, laws or by any man's religion. He can only be known through revelation – revelation as revealed in the Gospel and by the Holy Spirit.

Be mindful, unless God makes Himself known, He cannot be known. Unbelief is the worst enemy of man, so let us cast away every doubt, suspicion, and irreverence and readily accepts the word as presented:

> "Wherefore lay apart all filthiness and superfluity of naughtiness, and receive with meekness the engrafted word, which is able to save your souls" (James 1:21; cf. Romans 11:32).

Personally, I do not think there is any benefit for being an atheist. Any man who says he does not believe in God or accepts the sovereignty of the Creator definitely has something beside himself to believe and worship.

Every one of us to some extent is an idolater. We all have our little gods which we adore and worship knowingly or unknowingly. Examples of such insidious gods can be a child, spouse, parent, social standing, job and hobby, education, car, house, pet, and money. These things and persons in themselves may not be bad, but they can take the place of God.

Written for mankind, the Bible reveals God as being merciful to all, and especially those who take Him at His word. Jesus Christ is God's invitation letter calling every man to repent and be saved:

> **"Come now, and let us reason together, saith the LORD: though your sins be as scarlet, they shall be as white as snow; though they be red like crimson, they shall be as wool" (Isaiah 1:18).**

I hope this brief testimony of the connection between Jesus Christ and the Bible has been most helpful. Experience has revealed that where people have given up on the Bible as the absolute truth morality lapses. Men lose their sanity and unbelief replaces faith in God.

God is a buckler to them that trust His word:

> **"As for God, his way is perfect; the word of the LORD is tried: he is a buckler to all them that trust in him" (2 Samuel 22:31).**

There are three more hurdles to climb before I get to the main body of this book, so permit me to quickly take that out of the way in the next two chapters.

Chapter 2

THE GOD OF THE BIBLE

Jesus Christ will not be understood unless we first lay hold on the truth concerning the God of the Bible, who is the Creator and owner of the universe. God is a person and knowable. He is essentially one in His Being, but within this being there are three persons. God is Trinity (Trinitarian) – Three-in-one God:

"For there are three that bear record in heaven, the Father, the Word (Son), and the Holy Ghost: and these three are one" (1 John 5:7; John 1:1).

God presents Himself to man in three persons: The Father, the Son or the Word and the Holy Spirit. The Father is wholly God; the Son is wholly God, and the Holy Spirit is wholly God. Irrespective, there are not three God's, but one.

The three persons are self-distinctive in the one true God. The Father, Son and Spirit are one: Co-Creators, coeternal, and co-equal. All the persons of the trinity are referred to as, "He." It is a deviation from the Bible to make God feminine. → *Original language not discovered until 1945 would disagree.*

God is a pure Spirit of infinite perfections. As a pure Spirit, God is invisible: *Spirit is not a body.*

> "God is a Spirit: and they that worship him must worship him in spirit and truth" (John 4:24; Deuteronomy 4:15ff; Psalm 147:5; Isaiah 40:25-26).

Even though God does not have a human body or confined to matter, yet, He possesses all the attributes of personality such as life, Omniscience, foreknowledge, wisdom, self-consciousness, and self-manifestation. He thinks, speaks, wills, and acts (Genesis 1:3-4).

Although, not a human being, God possesses human features and members such as face, eyes, nostrils, organs of speech, shoulders, hand, fingers, back, feet, and uses human voice, grieves, jealous, uses weapons, gets angry, and takes vengeance (cf. Genesis 32:30; 2 Chronicles 16:9; 2 Samuel 22:9; Numbers 12:8; Psalm 2:4; Exodus 3:4; Jeremiah 50:25; Numbers 12:9; Hebrews 10:30).

That God is local and knowable is plain in Scripture. He is not far from any one of us: "for in him we live, and move, and have our being" (Acts 17:26-28). He is God of His covenant people, and also God of the nations. All that God needs man to know about Him are written in the Bible, and can be accepted on the basis of faith with the aid of the Holy Spirit.

In fact, there have been many instances in history where God made Himself known to man prior to His final revelation, Jesus Christ. The Bible records times when God appeared to man as a man, or in the form of man (cf. Genesis 18:1; 35:9; Exodus 24:9-11; Job 42:5; Isaiah 6:1; Ezekiel 1:26; Daniel 7:9; Revelations 4:2).

Enoch, for example, walked with God and was not. He was taken to heaven alive (Genesis 5:24). The patriarch Abraham was called the friend of God (Isaiah 41:8). God spoke to Moses "as a man speaks with his friend" (Exodus 33:11).

The God of the Bible is the God of the universe. He is God of nature as well as of religion, and of the secular as well as the sacred. Every good and perfect gift comes from Him: Music, recreation, friendship, sex, culture, marriage, family, beauty, the natural world, inter-racial inter-cultural communities, planes, boat, cars and the many others that enrich the quality of human life; it all comes from Him (cf. James 1:17).

Chapter 2: The God of the Bible

God has many names, but there is one peculiar name which He refers to as His personal or proper name – that name is "Yahweh (YHWH)" or "Jehovah (Lord)." This is the name whereby God reveals Himself to man.

Jehovah is the covenant name of God, who is immanent and who desires to be with His human creatures or man:

> "And God spake unto Moses, and said unto him, I am the LORD: And I appeared unto Abraham, unto Isaac, and unto Jacob, by the name of God Almighty, but by my name JEHOVAH was I not known to them" (Exodus 6:2-3; 3:13-14).

As the personal God, "Yahweh or Jehovah" is His personal name for all times (Exodus 3:15b). By assuming this divine name, God conveys to man that; He is not just the Creator but also God who is with His creation.

The God of the Bible does not just exist; He is with His people – God -with-us. He is the self-existing God who is with His people or who wants to be with His people at all times and everywhere.

God is the Creator of every human being, but He is also the Father of the redeemed (Deuteronomy 32:6; Mathew 6:9; 11:25; 1 Corinthians 8:6; Ephesians 3:14). Jesus Christ taught us to call God Father (Pater). Father solidifies our relationship to God and vice versa.

God is not far away, aloof, or unconcerned. By His Divine name (s) we know that God is indeed personal, sovereign, active, and separate from all others. His name (s) reveals who He is, what He has and what He does. God even requested that His people "prove" Him in tithing:

> "Bring ye all the tithes into the storehouse, that there may be meat in mine house, and prove me now herewith, saith the LORD of hosts, if I will not open you the windows of heaven, and pour you out a blessing, that there shall not be room enough to receive it" (Malachi 3:10).

To know the personal name of God is very important since His name proves His existence. His name is the name that man can trust and call upon at all times. Every man can know God because He has given us His name:

> **"They that know thy name will put their trust in thee: for thou, LORD, hast not forsaken them that seek thee (Psalm 9:10).**

> **"The name of the LORD is a strong tower: the righteous runneth into it, and is safe" (Proverbs 18:10).**

There are many descriptive names of the Father that directly applies to the Son such as: Creator, Redeemer, Wonderful, Counselor, The mighty God, and The Everlasting Father, which I shall discuss further down in this book.

Further, there are other names that are exclusively assigned to the Son such as Prince of Peace, Savior, Christ or the Anointed One, Word or the Word of God, Holy One, the Branch, King of Kings and Lord of Lords. Jesus the Christ or Jesus Christ is the name the Son of God assumed when He became a man – the name of the incarnate Son of God.

These names are indication of the equality and unity within the Godhead – Father, Son and Holy Spirit, share the same glory. For example, when you praise one, you have praised all. Below are few tips about the person of God for your personal studies.

They do not sum up who God is. They are attributes which rises from His nature and in His dealings with mankind. Some are attributes which constitutes His spiritual nature and character while others speaks of His absolute attributes which are His own inherent excellences:

1. Holy – God is, in His essence, by His nature, holiness itself. He is wholly "other." God is free from evil, hates and abhors sin and incapable of error. His holiness makes Him glorious. Holiness is His essence and He can never lose it. There is absolutely no unrighteousness in Him. Evil cannot survive in His presence.

Chapter 2: The God of the Bible

2. Righteous – holiness is His essence, and righteousness is the way by which His essence is expressed toward anything apart from Himself. God is what man's holiness and righteousness must be. His righteousness is the standard of conduct for all men for "there is none holy as the Lord." God is the moral governor of the universe (Exodus 3:5; 15:11; Leviticus 19:2; Deuteronomy 11:45; 1 Samuel 2:2; Isaiah 43:15; 1 Peter 1:15,16).

3. Love – God is love. His nature is love – He is love itself. Every act of God is the outcome of His love. The Bible is clear that God loves all His creatures. He is the Father of all who trust and obey Him (John 3:16; 4:10; 1 John 4:8,16). It was His love that made Him to create us in His own image and likeness. Man is unique, even his body, is made to house God (1 Corinthians 6:19). Again, it is His love that sent His only begotten Son to earth to die for all (Romans 5:8).

4. Just – He is just and righteous. He is God of justification as well as justice. He always does what is right. God will surely punish sin, but He would also reward righteousness. Therefore, man has the choice to accept the sacrifice of God's Son and be acquitted from sin or face everlasting hell as alternative as punishment for sin (Mark 10:18; Deuteronomy 32:4; Psalm 89:14; 92:15; 2 Corinthians 5:21; Mathew 5:45).

5. Good – He is essentially good. Good is the old English word for God. God's goodness makes Him deal kindly and bountifully with all His creatures. Why this earth has lasted for this long despite man's depravity and wickedness is due to God's goodness (Genesis 1:31, Psalm 25:8; 33:6; 118:29; 145:9; Mathew 5:45).

6. Merciful – God is full of mercy. The mercy of God provided His Son as the Sacrificial Lamb for sin. God

does not even punish us as we deserve when we sin. All his judgments and punishment for sin and sins are mitigated. God is longsuffering (Exodus 34:6; Deuteronomy 4:31; Romans 9:11-15; 2 Timothy 1:9; 2 Peter 3:9). His delight is not the death of the sinner.

7. Faithful – His promises are good. The faithfulness of God manifests itself in His longsuffering towards us. His faithfulness supplies and sustains the earth and man. He does not forsake His creatures. He is our helper in times of trials, temptations and afflictions (2 Peter 3:9; Romans 2:4; Lamentations 3:23; Mathew 28:20; Philippians 4:19)

8. Jealous – He hates and abhors every form of idolatry. God has no room for rivals and neither does He share His glory with any other. There is no God beside Yahweh the Lord. God is also very jealous for His people. He that touches His saints "touches the apple of his eye." (Exodus 20:5; 34:14; Deuteronomy 4:23-24; Zechariah 2:8; James 4:5). He alone deserves the praise, glory and the labor of all His creatures.

9. Truthful – God is intrinsically truthful. He deals truthfully with all His creatures. It is impossible for God to lie. As the only True God and the moral governor of the universe, He demands truth from all creatures without exception. Jesus Christ is the truth and the way into truth. "God is light, and in him is no darkness at all" (1 John 1:5). The Holy Spirit is the Spirit of truth and the dispenser of truth (Deuteronomy 32:4; Psalm 51:6; 89:37; John 14:6; Titus 1:2; Hebrews 6:18).

10. Impartial – He has no favorites. God is without partiality (Job 36:5; Deuteronomy 10:17; Acts 10:34; Romans 2:6,11; James 3:17; 1 Peter 1:17). "Wherefore now let the fear of the LORD be upon you; take heed and do it: for there is no iniquity with the LORD

our God or respect of persons, nor taking of gifts" (2 Chronicles 19:7).

11. Irresistible – no creature can hinder Him. It is pure folly to pick up quarrel with God. It is absolutely impossible to resist Him (Numbers 23:20; Job 9:12; Ecclesiastes 1:15; 6:10; 7:13; Isaiah 43:13; Daniel 4:35). God stands alone in absolute authority and power.

12. Incomparable – He is of the "other." There is no god like Him in moral character and in all His attributes (Exodus 15:11; Deuteronomy 33:26; Psalm 113:4-6; Isaiah 40:13; 55:8-9; Lamentations 3:37). All depends on Him, but He depends on no one. He is self-existing.

13. Savior – He alone can save to the uttermost. He alone has the power to save man from sin, Satan's power and the wrath to come upon the disobedient forever. God is a judge and a Savior. "I, even I, am the LORD; and beside me there is no savior" (Isaiah 43:11). Jesus Christ came into this world to sinners (1 Timothy 1:15).

14. Omnipresent – He is everywhere. He fills all creation. God is present universally and simultaneously in every part of His universe (Jeremiah 23:23-24; Psalm 139:7-10; Numbers 14:21; Isaiah 66:1; Acts 7:48-49).

15. Unchangeable – He is immutable. His perfections, promises, purposes are forever the same. In His person God is unchangeable, but His relationship towards His creatures changes depending on how we respond to him and to His commandments (cf. Ezekiel 33:13-16). Though His actions may vary according to our conduct, He Himself does not change. He does not have swing moods (Numbers 23:19; 1 Samuel 15:29; Psalms 33:11; Malachi 3:6; Hebrews 6:17; James 1:17).

16. Immense – He is everywhere. His center is everywhere; His circumference is nowhere (2 Chronicles 6:18. Time and space is within His immensity.

17. Eternal – He never began to live; He has always lived. His existence excludes any measurement of time. His name "I am," connotes pure existence. He ever lives to make good His purposes and promises (Genesis 1:1; Psalm 9:7; 90:2; 93:2; 102:12,24-27; Exodus 3:14; Deuteronomy 32:40; Isaiah 41:4; 57:15).

18. Self-Sufficient – He has no need. All creatures; angels, man and animals depend on Him for existence, but He Himself is unconscious of need (Psalm 50:12; Acts 17:24; Romans 11:35-36).

19. Self-Existence – He is Jehovah or the great "I AM." God is life. He has life in Himself and independent of everything about Himself. He is the source and preserver of all life. He does not depend on any creature for existence, joy and counsel.

20. Omnipotent – He is the "All Powerful One." Nothing is too hard for Him. However, there are some things God cannot do such as lie, sin or deny Himself. God cannot act contrary to His nature (Jeremiah 32:17-18,27; Exodus 15:6; Numbers 23:19; Luke 1:37; 2 Timothy 2:13). He is fully in control of the world and all the events unfolding before us today.

21. Omniscient – He knows all things. God is all-knowing. He knows what is going on at all times in all places. He knows the end of all things from the beginning. He has intuitive, simultaneous, infallible perceptions of Himself, all creatures and the physical universe. He knows exactly how and when He would end the world (Psalm 33:13-14; 139:11-12; 147:5; Proverbs 5:21; 15:3; Romans 11:33; 1 John 3:20).

Chapter 2: The God of the Bible

22. The Living God – Jesus Christ is the sum of the father's will and purpose. In Him dwelleth the fullness of the Godhead bodily. He is the visible expression of the invisible God. In Him, God is fully revealed as the living God (John 1:1-3,14; 14:6; Proverbs 8:30).

23. Unity – there is only one God. The Hebrew word for one denotes a compound unity and not a single unity (cf. Genesis 2:4; 11:6; 1 Corinthians 12:13; Galatians 3:28). However, there is no competition whatsoever within the Godhead, instead they heap praise on each other (2 Corinthians 13:14). When you see or know one, you have seen and know all.

24. Free – He is answerable to no one but Himself. The laws of nature or the universe are subservient to Him. He transcends every law – no matter whose law. He controls all the powers of nature and makes them serve His purpose. He can change, stop, remove or do without any of His laws as He sees fit. He is obligated to no one, but all creatures are obligated to Him. God always does what is good and right. He cannot do evil.

Jesus Christ commanded His followers to baptize those who believe in Him in the name of trinity. All that is true about God is also true of the Son and the Holy Spirit:

> **"Go ye therefore, and teach all nations, baptizing them in the name of the Father, and of the Son, and of the Holy Ghost"** (Mathew 28:18; cf. Exodus 33:20; John 1:1,14; Acts 5:3,4; 2 Corinthians 13:14; Revelations 1:4-5).

The truth about God may transcend our reason but surely does not contradict it. The word of God is absolute truth and above the unaided mind; however, they can be readily accepted and understood by faith through Jesus Christ in the Holy Spirit. Let me illustrate what I have just said. We all know in mathematics that one plus one equals two. But with God, one plus one may not always add up to two. It could be one, two hundred, or even one thousand to say the least.

[Handwritten note: Jesus' parables reveal that God doesn't "see" as we see. We are not expected to understand.]

Although God created time and the seasons, He Himself is not bound by time. There are no time divisions with God – past, present, and future are all in the present to Him and with Him. God transcends time. Further, there is no law above God, but there is law in God.

Unfortunately, I may have to stop here, but here is a brief summary on this awesome God of the Bible. He is God the Father, the Son and the Holy Spirit. The Father is the source of all things. All things come through the Son and by the Holy Spirit. Under the Old Testament, men "called upon the name of the Lord" (cf. Genesis 4:26; 12:8; 1 Kings 18:24; Psalm 79:6; Isaiah 6:47). Under the New Testament, men are advised to "call upon the name of the Lord Jesus Christ" (cf. Acts 9:14,21; 22:16; 1 Corinthians 1:2; 2 Timothy 2:22).

Chapter 3

DATELESS PAST

To Know Jesus Christ before His incarnation (before He became a man) is extremely essential because He is very much connected to the dateless past. By the phrase, 'dateless past,' I mean, before the worlds were made and before the beginning of the human race and before the beginning of history.

Jesus Christ would not make sense unless He is understood from His connection with eternity past. Who Jesus was before He became a man is essential to ease some of the misunderstandings that has plagued the minds of many for centuries.

A sound knowledge of Jesus Christ from the dateless past would give you a clearer and broader view to re-examine Him. An understanding of what was done or put in place through Him before creation began would provide a greater appreciation of His representative and redemption role in history.

The purpose of God is in Jesus Christ or is Jesus Christ. Every action of God arises out of His eternal purpose. Because God has absolute knowledge of all things, and knows the end of all things from the beginning, He plans out everything from start to finish before He begins.

The nature of the universe and how the world of humanity would function and be governed were long established before creation actually began. God sees the end from start and tells the future from the present. Whatever God does is forever:

> "Remember the former things of old: for I am God, and there is none else; I am God, and there is none like me.
>
> Declaring the end from the beginning, and from ancient times the things that are not yet done, saying, My counsel shall stand, and I will do all my pleasure" (Isaiah 46:9-10).

According to the Bible, before the beginning of all things including man, Jesus dwelt with God as the Eternal Word. This pre-incarnation existence underlies most of his self-revealed statements like the two below:

> "What and if ye shall see the Son of man ascend up where he was before?" (John 6:62)
>
> "And now, O Father, glorify thou me with thine own self with the glory which I had with thee before the world was" (John 17:5).

As the eternal Word, both man and things were created by His decision and through His action. Further, Jesus Christ is the reason for creation: "For of him, and through him, and to him are all things" (Romans 11:36):

> "For by him were all things created, that are in heaven, and that are in earth, visible and invisible, whether they be thrones, or dominions, or principalities, or powers: all things were created by him, and for him" (Colossians 1:16).

As the eternal Word and the Son, He is self-existent. Our world is Christo-centric. For by Him, for His use, and for His glory the universe was made. Creation stands created because of Him. He is the first born of every creature – the head of all creation:

> "Who is the image of the invisible God, the firstborn of every creature" (Colossians 1:15).

Chapter 3: Dateless Past

Be mindful, Jesus is the firstborn, not the first created. Firstborn signifies priority of time. It speaks of His sovereignty and pre-existence – what He was from eternity. He existed before all creation. He was not a part of creation, but apart from creation.

According to the Scriptures, before man and his world were made, God appointed Jesus Christ as the Savior of the human race. By His foreknowledge, God put in place a plan that would justify and redeem man from sin, His wrath and death in history.

God was fully aware of what would become of man shortly after he is created; therefore, He appointed His only Son Jesus Christ as His rescue plan – as a redeemer and propitiation for the sin and sins of mankind (Exodus 15:2; Psalm 27:1).

According to the eternal plan, Jesus Christ would come to earth from heaven as the last Adam and as the representative humanity (second man) at an appointed time in history. He would come after sin is introduced into the world and the fall of the first man Adam:

> "And so it is written, the first man Adam was made a living soul; the last Adam was made a quickening spirit. Howbeit that was not first which is spiritual, but that which is natural; and afterward that which is spiritual. The first man is of the earth, earthy; the second man is the Lord from heaven" (1 Corinthians 15:45-47).

By His foreknowledge and sovereignty, God at this dateless past determined that any man who places his trust or faith in the vicarious and expiatory sacrifice of His Son Jesus Christ shall be declared righteous (justified) by grace through faith:

> "Whoever believeth on Him shall not be ashamed" (Romans 9:33b).

The wages of sin is death, according to the law of God; therefore, there cannot be remission of sins without the shedding of blood (Hebrews 9:22; Romans 3:25). God chose

Jesus Christ as His "gift of life" to fallen man – life begets life. God gave the life of His Son to save the lives of His human creatures:

> "Who verily was foreordained before the foundation of the world, but was manifest in this last times for you" (1 Peter 1:20; cf. John 17:24).

Sin as a rebellion and a reproach to God and is punishable by death. But, due to the mercy and the grace of God, at this pre-creation and pre-crucifixion era, the blood of Jesus Christ was spiritually shed for the remission of sins yet to be committed.

In the sight of God, Jesus Christ – the Lamb of God was slain in anticipation of His death on the Cross of Calvary in history:

> "The Lamb slain from the foundation of the world" (Revelation 13:8b).

The redemption of man was hid in the cross. Death through sin would be over-ruled by His death and His resurrection would make new life available to all who choose to belief in history. Thankfully, these divine arrangements were unknown to Satan, the arc-enemy of the human race. Had he known, he would not have instigated the death of Jesus Christ:

> "Which none of the princes of this world knew: for had they known it, they would not have crucified the Lord of glory" (1 Corinthians 2:8).

Man cannot live without dying, so eternal life cannot come to man without death to sin. Gratefully, "If Jesus died for all, then were all dead." All who belief Him die in His death and are given new life by His resurrection (2 Corinthians 5:14):

> "Him, being delivered by the determinate counsel and foreknowledge of God, ye have taken, and by wicked hands have crucified and slain" (Acts 2:23).

Pre-creation shed blood of Jesus Christ was the reason God was able to forgive sins committed prior to Calvary. The sins

Chapter 3: Dateless Past

committed four thousand years prior to the death on the cross of Calvary.

The Old Testament ordinances and sacrifices were permitted for the purpose of educating sin ridden man on the indispensable nature of the blood of Jesus Christ in the expiation of sins. It was His blood that atoned for the sins of humanity (Leviticus 17:11).

This shed blood was the reason the blood of bulls and goat were accepted for the expiation of sin during that short period of time in history for the people of Israel. God forgave the sins of Israel under the old dispensation not necessarily for the blood of innocent bulls and goat, but the shed blood of the Lamb of God "slain from the foundation of the world" (Revelation 13:8):

> **"For it is not possible that the blood of bulls and of goats should take away sins" (Hebrews 10:5).**

The same rule applies to us who live in this Post-Calvary dispensation. God looks at the blood of His Son to grant forgiveness and salvation to all who express the need and exercise faith in His Son.

Also, at this dateless past, Jesus Christ was appointed heir of all things – the life and prosperity of the human race were firmly secured in His hands. He was appointed as the King of Kings and the Lord of Lords in anticipation of His victory over sin, Satan and death (Revelations 19:16).

The eternal purpose of God is that, in the "fullness of times" God would gather the whole universe under Christ:

> **"That in the dispensation of the fullness of times he might gather together in one all things in Christ, both which are in heaven, and which are on earth; even in him" (Ephesians 1:10; cf. Romans 8:21).**

'Times,' in the above quotation is in the plural because it covers the period of Christ first advent, the present age, His second advent, millennium reign, the judgment seat of Christ, the judgment at the great white throne and the ages thereafter.

It extends into the period of sinless and endless glory under the reign of Jesus Christ (cf. 2 Corinthians 5:10; Ephesians 2:7; Revelations 22:3).

Certainly, it was befitting that the one by whom all things were made and the one by whom the human race and the world shall be saved be made heir of all things. God is infinite in wisdom, and may His holy name be forever praised:

"God, who at sundry times and in divers manners spake in times past unto the fathers by the prophets, hath in this last days spoken to us by his Son, whom he hath appointed heir of all things, by whom also he made the worlds" (Hebrews 1:1-2; cf. Mathew 28:18).

The church at this dateless past was also chosen in Him with their names written in the "Book of Life" (Revelations 13:8; 17:8). The church was chosen to be His body, His bride, temple and joint-heirs. They were chosen to reign with Him.

According to these eternal arrangements, and by the principle of election, individuals elected to reign with Jesus Christ would be made the sons of God in history. They would be adopted as sons of God in Jesus Christ (cf. Ephesians 1:5; Romans 8:28-29).

The word 'adoption' does not have the same meaning as the English version; i.e., the taking of an orphan to be ones' own child. In Ephesians 1:5, it means the public recognition, attestation or placement of adult sonship.

The holiness to which these individuals were chosen: "Is to be without blame before God in love" (cf. Ephesians 1:4; cf. 2 Timothy 2:9,19) "Eternal life' or the 'righteousness that only God provides for all men through Jesus Christ' would be available to all persons who put their faith and hope in His incarnate Son of God:

"According as he has chosen us in him before the foundation of the world that we should be holy and without blame before him in love" (Ephesians 1:4).

Chapter 3: Dateless Past

"Beloved, now we are the sons of God, and it doth not yet appear what we shall be: but we know that, when he shall appear, we shall be like him; for we shall see him as he is" (1 John 3:2).

The proof of sonship and belonging to God would be the indwelling Holy Spirit Himself (Romans 8:9b). They would be sealed with the Holy Spirit as God's very own. Born again and Spirit led, the sons of God would be able to live as the salt and light with power on earth in history:

"But as many as received him, to them gave he power to become the sons of God, even to them that believe on his name" (John 1:12).

"In whom ye also trusted, after that you heard the word of truth, the gospel of your salvation: in whom also after that ye believed, ye were sealed with the Holy Spirit of promise" (Ephesians 1:13).

The church, made up of both Old and New Testament saints, Jews and Gentiles, were at this pre-creation era chosen to be God's very own – chosen to be a peculiar treasure (1 Peter 2:9). God fore-chose and fore-fixed the destiny and the inheritance of the church from the beginning of creation:

"Then shall the King say unto them on his right hand, Come, ye blessed of my Father, inherit the kingdom prepared for you from the foundation of the world" (Mathew 25:34).

"In whom also we have obtained an inheritance, being predestinated according purpose of him who worketh all things after the counsel of his own will" (Ephesians 1:11).

History may set the age of the church at two thousand years, but it pre-dates history. The church was chosen in Christ before the earth was made and before Israel was chosen in history (Acts 7:38).

Again, embodied in these dateless arrangements was the restoration of all things by Jesus Christ. At a future great event known as the glorification of the sons of God, creation or nature shall be delivered from its current bondage to corruption.

Through the one-time sacrifice of Jesus Christ, damage to nature as a result of sin and the wickedness of mankind shall be done away with forever. Through Him, God would reconcile unto Himself all things in His universe – things in heaven, on earth and under the earth (Colossians 1:19).

Beloved, can you, from all that you have read so far, see the wisdom of God? His ways are past finding. God is not only powerful and omniscience, but infinitely wise. God operates unspent. He never sleeps nor slumbers and is immutable. Here is a Bible quotation I have come to love and respect. I pray you do the same:

> "Who hath measured the waters in the hollow of his hand, and meted out heaven with the span, and comprehended the dust of the earth in a measure, and weighed the mountains in scales, and the hills in a balance?
>
> Who hath directed the Spirit of the LORD, or being his counsellor hath taught him? With whom took he counsel, and who instructed him, and taught him in the path of judgment, and taught him knowledge, and shewed to him the way of understanding?
>
> Behold, the nations are as a drop of a bucket, and are counted as the small dust of the balance: behold, he taketh up the isles as a very little thing. To whom then will ye liken God? or what likeness will ye compare unto him?
>
> Have ye not known? have ye not heard? hath it not been told you from the beginning? have ye not understood from the foundations of the earth?

Chapter 3: Dateless Past

It is he that sitteth upon the circle of the earth, and the inhabitants thereof are as grasshoppers; that stretcheth out the heavens as a curtain, and spreadeth them out as a tent to dwell in: To whom then will ye liken me, or shall I be equal? saith the Holy One" (Isaiah 40:12-15,18,21,22,25).

All that was needed to secure eternal salvation and redemption for mankind were at this dateless past completed and sealed before creation began. In the sight of Him, who "Calls things which be not as though they were, the order of things were forever set even before man was formed and made (cf. Romans 4:17).

But, the surprise concerning these eternal pre-creation arrangements is that, anyone who reads the bible even for the first time would not take long to notice that none of these are openly revealed in the creation chapters of the Bible.

In the first two chapters of the creation narratives (Genesis chapters 1 and 2), God rested from all His labors on the seventh day without any mention of His dateless arrangements. The reason, they were kept secret in Christ with God. Why? Here is the Bible answer:

"And to make all men see what is the fellowship of the mystery, which from the beginning of the world hath been hid in God, who created all things by Jesus Christ. According to the eternal purpose which he purposed in Christ Jesus our Lord" (Ephesians 3:9,11; cf. verses 1-12).

"To the intent that now unto the principalities and powers in heavenly places might be known by the church the manifold wisdom of God" (Ephesians 3:10).

They were kept secret in Christ with God to be revealed at the appointed time. The apostle Paul rightly calls them 'mystery:'

"Even the mystery which hath been hid from ages and from generations, but now is made manifest to his saints" (Colossians 1:26).

"Now to him that is of power to establish you according to the gospel, and the preaching of Jesus Christ, according to the revelation of the mystery, which was kept secret since the world begun" (Romans 16:25).

The good news is that they are no longer secrets or mysteries because they have been revealed. The prophets of old prophesied that Jesus Christ when he comes to earth would utter" things which have been kept secret from the foundation of the world" (cf. Mathew 13:35b).

He would speak of things which were put in place by God before the world began. And this is the Gospel we preach from the Bible and write about – like this book:

"But we speak the wisdom of God in a mystery, even the hidden wisdom, which God ordained before the world unto our glory" (1 Corinthians 2:7).

The present chaos and rebellion of mankind is no surprise at all to God. God is still the sovereign God. He has not lost control of His universe. To be more candid and truthful, man would not end the world, only God can, but He has chosen not to.

Instead, God would bring every human word and deed to judgment, punish the wicked, reward the righteous and restore the earth to its former beauty and glory. The world would never end; it shall be restored to its premier glory and beyond at God's own appointed time.

Then, from henceforth, the universe would continue forever in righteousness and truth under the reign of Jesus Christ and God:

"And I saw a new heaven and a new earth: for the first heaven and the first earth were passed away; and there was no more sea (cf. Revelation 21:1).

Chapter 3: Dateless Past

Unfortunately, I may have to stop here and then complete the last hurdle on why Jesus Christ did not come to earth as God, instead took our human nature and became a man. But, before I do that, here is a brief summary.

God in His infinite wisdom and foreknowledge prior to the creation of the worlds appointed Jesus Christ as the last Adam, and the only Savior of His would-be human race through the first man Adam. Spiritually, creation and the order of things were all completed long before any one of them physically came into being.

Notes

Chapter 4

WHY GOD BECAME A MAN

Man has a beginning. Six days is given for the creation of the earth and its contents as you may learn more from the next chapter. God looked over all that He had made, and being completely satisfied stamped His approval declaring them: "Very good:"

"And God saw every thing that he had made, and, behold, it was very good. And the evening and the morning were the sixth day. (Genesis 1:31).

Man was the last to be formed and made in the six day creation event (cf. Hebrews 4:12; 1 Thessalonians 5:23). The creation of man – his whole body, soul and spirit were formed and made on the sixth day. On the seventh day God and man rested:

"Thus the heavens and the earth were finished, and all the host of them. And on the seventh day God ended his work which he had made; and he rested on the seventh day from all his work which he had made" (Genesis 2:1-2).

Man was purposely designed. Trinity (the three-in-one God), deliberated over the nature of the creature to be created and concluded to make man in "His own image and likeness." The fact that God the Son was willing to become a man and to die on a shameful cross to save mankind shows how important man was and still is to God:

> "And God said, Let us make man in our image, after our likeness: and let them have dominion over the fish of the sea, and over the fowl of the air, and over the cattle, and over all the earth, and over every creeping thing that creepeth upon the earth. So God created man in his own image, in the image of God created he him; male and female created he them" (Genesis 1:26.

It was God's idea to create man and He did create man male and female. First, God created the first male adult named Adam, and out of the man made the first female adult. Both male and female were created in the likeness and image of God on the same day. They were created equal but not identical. Man was upright from the moment he was made. His way of thinking, feeling, and acting was wholly conformed to the righteousness of God (cf. Ecclesiastes 7:29).

God created man for His own pleasure, and gave him the responsibility to work or manage the earth on His behalf (cf. Revelations 4:11). God entrusted man with the care of His planet earth immediately after he was made. As a result of this partnership, we can to some extent say, the earth rightly belongs to God but it also belongs to man.

Further, we can say, as far as the earth is concerned, man is second to God. Further, this appointment as the sole custodian of the earth means no outsider can do anything on earth without the permission of both God and man. God would not do anything on earth without man and man would not do anything without God.

Further still, man can only take instructions from his gracious Maker. Even after the fall of man, this order of things and line of leadership was upheld in Christ:

> "The head of every man is Christ; and the head of the woman is the man; and the head of Christ is God" (1 Corinthians 11:3; cf. Amos 3:7).

Man is to dominate all things, God said. The extent of the dominion, we may not know, but we see glimpses in the life of Adam before the fall, and the life and ministry of the incarnate Son of God. Angels, holy and fallen (Satan and his host of demons), cannot do anything on earth without the permission of God's sub-regent, man; this earth was legally closed to other beings or outsiders.

Again, God blessed man with the power of fruitfulness. Through this blessing, man can multiply, subdue the earth and take good care of the lower creatures under his control such as the fish, birds, and animals. The earth as a home to all earthly creatures means it is part of man's duty to ensure that the lower creatures are protected and cared for:

"And God blessed them, and God said unto them, Be fruitful, and multiply, and replenish the earth, and subdue it: and have dominion over the fish of the sea, and over the fowl of the air, and over every living thing that moveth upon the earth" (Genesis 1:28).

Finally, created man was put under probation. Longevity for him depended upon obedience to the divine command. Man was under restrictive divine command not to sin – he is not free to sin. Remember, evil cannot survive in the presence of the absolute holy God.

Even though man was created a free moral agent, temptation was permitted. His continuous existence in blissfulness, freedom and blessedness depends entirely upon his reaction to the divine prohibition. With the exception of the one tree – the tree of the knowledge of good and evil, man was free to eat of every edible tree in the Garden of Eden including the Tree of Life:

"And the LORD God commanded the man, saying, Of every tree of the garden thou mayest freely eat: But of the tree of the knowledge of good and evil, thou shalt not eat of it: for in the day that thou eatest thereof thou shalt surely die" (Genesis 2:15-16; cf. Deuteronomy 28).

The third chapter of the book of Genesis clearly states that Adam and Eve failed the test of probation. Adam and Eve, parents of the human race broke God's commandment. "The laws of God are the directions on the package of life." Mankind through Adam chose to disobey and by so doing chose death instead of life.

Even though, man as he was created possessed the ability not to sin, our first parents willfully chose to obey the evil counsel of Satan the tempter. The fall of man is a historical reality. Humanity by this deliberate act of willful disobedience became sinners. Our first parents fell into sin and became slave to sin:

> "**Know ye not, that to whom ye yield yourselves servants to obey, his servants ye are to whom ye obey; whether of sin unto death, or of obedience unto righteousness?**" (Romans 6:16).

The event of the fall is the darkest day in the history of mankind. The parents of the human race chose death instead of life, evil instead of good, bondage instead of freedom and their choice was for them and for us (descendants). By the fall, man lost the right to be himself. Man became naked, ashamed and fled from the presence of God his only Creator.

We all die because of the fall. By obeying Satan man became his servants: "You become servant to whom you choose to obey." Further, by this wicked act of our first parents, the entire human race sinned against God. Sin is evil.

The complex contradictions between man and God, husband and wife, and between man and nature, appeared as the consequence of sin. Sickness, disease, poverty, greed, human slavery, evil thoughts, evil desires, rape, murder, self-righteousness, self-religion, devotion to idols and all lying and wickedness have their root to man's corrupt nature handed down through birth from the fall (Romans 3:23; Psalm 51:5; 58:3).

By the fall, a silent world stood before the Creator guilty and punishable by death. Every attempt of man to establish his own righteousness before God is ruled out:

Chapter 4: Why God Became a Man

"Wherefore, as by one man sin entered into the world, and death by sin; and so death passed upon all men, for that all have sinned" (Romans 5:12).

But someone may ask; how did it all happen? In short, Satan from another part of God's creation entered this earth disguised as a serpent or clothed as a serpent and a creature of the earth and thus belonging to the earth, managed to deceive the first lady of the earth, and then Adam followed. Here is the account:

"Now the serpent was more subtil than any beast of the field which the LORD God had made. And he said unto the woman, Yea, hath God said, Ye shall not eat of every tree of the garden?

And the woman said unto the serpent, We may eat of the fruit of the trees of the garden: But of the fruit of the tree which is in the midst of the garden, God hath said, Ye shall not eat of it, neither shall ye touch it, lest ye die.

And the serpent said unto the woman, Ye shall not surely die: For God doth know that in the day ye eat thereof, then your eyes shall be opened, and ye shall be as gods, knowing good and evil.

And when the woman saw that the tree was good for food, and that it was pleasant to the eyes, and a tree to be desired to make one wise, she took of the fruit thereof, and did eat, and gave also unto her husband with her; and he did eat" (Genesis 3:1-6).

The presence of the two trees meant temptation was permitted; however, there was no need for them to fail. Man was well informed and prepared for the test. Temptation for man is always subject to the human will and desires (James 1:14-15; cf. Genesis 4:7). Every test or temptation is tailored. It is what a man can bear or handle.

Eve was deceived into disobedience, but her husband Adam was not. He willingly followed her disobedience (cf. Romans 5:12-14; 1 Timothy 2:14). Although, both were culpable, the Bible places the event of the fall squarely on Adam.

Adam and Eve sinned against God by their own free will. Sin when acted upon becomes a state. We are sinners by nature and sinners by choice. Our inherited corrupt nature is the reason we all sin without exception. Man is unable not to sin (cf. Romans 3). As a result of the fall, man is not as he was made; his nature is corrupt and rotten to the core and is perishing.

Sin is taking your eyes away from God; sin is to trust something, someone plus God; sin is a mistake; Sin is a lie; sin is missing the mark; sin is a trespass of divine limits; sin is a principle; sin is death; sin is a contradiction and a confusion. Further, sin is destructive of all good – it is an act against the goodness and grace of God. Sin is immoral and irrational. Only fools make a mockery of sin (cf. Proverbs 14:9).

Like Adam and Eve, existence for each of us depends upon our obedience to the word of God. Liberty without law is license and responsibility without freedom is bondage. Life for man is obedience to God's command; likewise, disobedience is death. A fact we may not agree with is the fact that; naturally, every man hates God and rejects His rule.

The sad part of it all is that, to date many people still prefer the evil ways of Satan to the righteous ways of God. Many people choose to follow both ways, but here is the truth: "No man can serve two masters: "for either he will hate the one, and love the other; or else he will hold to the one, and despise the other" (Mathew 6:24).

Satan came into this world through a lie and holds man in bondage through a lie. Through deception and by the permission of man, Satan and his host of fallen angels and demons entered the world and still occupy the world. Satan is still active in the world by the will of man.

Satan is said to be the father of the unregenerate because man chooses to obey his voice and to follow his evil ways. I hope

Chapter 4: Why God Became a Man

you can now understand why Jesus said the following about fallen man:

> "Ye are of your father the devil, and the lusts of your father ye will do. He was a murderer from the beginning, and abode not in the truth, because there is no truth in him. When he speaketh a lie, he speaketh of his own: for he is a liar, and the father of it" (John 8:44).

Here is a summary of the indictment against the human race for your study (cf. Psalm 14; Romans 3:10-18):

1. There is none righteous, no, not one. Righteousness is the criterion by which sin is judged.
2. There is none that understandeth, there is none that seeketh after God. Naturally man hates.
3. All gone out of the way, they are together become unprofitable; there is none that doeth good, no, not one.
4. Their throat is an open sepulchre; with their tongues they have used deceit; the poison of asps is under their lips.
5. Whose mouth is full of cursing and bitterness.
6. Their feet are swift to shed blood.
7. Destruction and misery are in their ways.
8. And the way of peace have they not known.
9. There is no fear of God before their eyes.

The whole world is bound to plead guilty before at God's tribunal; no man can expect to be justified there on the grounds of his own works, and not even by being obedience to the law of God. What man desperately need is a new birth or imputed righteousness. The divine law requires righteousness from every man without exception.

But, then, how may a man be justified, or declared righteous? If God requires righteousness and if man is a sinner or a transgressor, how can he stand before his holy God? Man cannot save himself. As a result of the fall, man is beyond repair and only rebirth can give him a new start and a clean slate.

Man needs a new nature. He needs a transformation and not a reformation. To bring about that, man needs someone outside himself to plead his case before God. Man needs a substitute to assume his guilt and punishment. Unfortunately, angels cannot stand in for man, they are fallible themselves.

The only way out is for God to enter man's world and save man and nature or else man is lost forever. The wages sin pays is death – man sinned, man must die. By man sin and death are in this world by man also it must be eradicated and destroyed:

"For since by man came death, by man came also the resurrection of the dead" (1 Corinthians 15:21).

Graciously, God chose to enter man's world to save him. As already mentioned, an eternal plan was already in place to save man from sin and death. Man can be declared righteous or justified through the substitutionary death of the incarnate Son of God Jesus Christ. Here is the divine testimony:

"And I looked, and there was none to help; and I wondered that there was none to uphold: therefore mine own arm brought salvation unto me; and my fury, it upheld me" (Isaiah 63:5; cf. John 3:16).

Righteous living is life, peace and joy for every man. Conformity to God's righteousness is the only means by which man can experience the highest felicity for which his nature is created. Let me briefly explain what Biblical righteousness is.

The "righteousness of God" or "justification" is a legal declaration issued by God in which He pronounces a person free from quilt. To justify means 'to pronounce and treat as righteous." Pardon and mere forgiveness from God is not enough to pay for the damage done through the fall. Let me use this illustration to show you how the righteousness of God works:

"You may wrong me and come to me; and I may say, I forgive you. But I have not justified you. I cannot justify you. But when God justifies a man, He says, 'I pronounce you a righteous man.' Henceforth I am going to treat you as if you never committed any sin."

Now, tell me, does this sound like something man can achieve or do by self-efforts or merit? The answer is absolutely no. The only way this much needed kind of righteousness can come to any man is through "the grace and mercy of God."

The only way God can justify the ungodly without any infringement to His own absolute holiness is true His substitute man Jesus Christ. God cannot act against His nature. He cannot overlook sin and neither would He "acquit the wicked."

Through Jesus Christ, God is able to "justify" all those who come to Him for salvation. He is able brings them into a right relationship with Himself while remaining perfectly righteous. In Christ, God does the very thing which in the law He says He would not do (cf. Exodus 23:7). Jesus Christ is God's only answer to man's precarious and hopeless situation:

> "But now the righteousness of God without the law is manifested, being witnessed by the law and the prophets; Even the righteousness of God which is by faith of Jesus Christ unto all and upon all them that believe: for there is no difference:
>
> For all have sinned, and come short of the glory of God; Being justified freely by his grace through the redemption that is in Christ Jesus: Whom God hath set forth to be a propitiation through faith in his blood, to declare his righteousness for the remission of sins that are past, through the forbearance of God;
>
> To declare, I say, at this time his righteousness: that he might be just, and the justifier of him which believeth in Jesus.

Jesus Christ is where God meets man – our "Mercy Seat." He is every man's reconciliatory and mediator. The expiation which is provided in Christ averts the wrath of God and wipes out the sinners guilt:

> **"Behold the Lamb of God, which taketh away the sin of the world" (John 1:29).**

Today, all generations can rejoice for the fact that God has done exactly what He planned out to do from the beginning. Both the Bible and history bear witness to the truth that, at the appointed time, Jesus Christ the Son of God entered the world not as God or an angel, but as a complete or full man through the lineage of first man Adam, but without sin.

The testimony of the Bible is that, two thousand years ago, Jesus Christ, who was in the form of God, in the incarnation, "emptied" Himself and took on our human nature and "tasted death for every man" (Hebrews 2:9):

> **"Let this mind be in you, which was also in Christ Jesus: Who, being in the form of God, thought it not robbery to be equal with God: But made himself of no reputation, and took upon him the form of a servant, and was made in the likeness of men: And being found in fashion as a man, he humbled himself, and became obedient unto death, even the death of the cross" (Philippians 2:5-11).**

While He was fully God, Jesus became fully man to experience death for every man. He assumed the guilt and punishment for our sin and sins. He never ceased to be God while He was on earth, but He chose not to exercise His prerogatives as God. He lived among us as one of us and even became the servant of all men.

Here is another reason for the incarnation. Since the people Jesus had to save were men subject to death, He, the Son of God, also became like one of us (the Son of man) so that through death He can destroy the works of Satan and deliver man from bondage:

> "Forasmuch then as the children are partakers of flesh and blood, he also himself likewise took part of the same; that through death he might destroy him that had the power of death, that is, the devil.
>
> And deliver them who through fear of death were all their lifetime subject to bondage. For verily he took not on him the nature of angels; but he took on him the seed of Abraham.
>
> Wherefore in all things it behoved him to be made like unto his brethren, that he might be a merciful and faithful high priest in things pertaining to God, to make reconciliation for the sins of the people.
>
> For in that he himself hath suffered being tempted, he is able to succour them that are tempted" (Hebrews 2:16-18).

Humanity under first man Adam failed, but the new humanity, under Jesus Christ, the last man Adam, did not fail and would not fail. First man Adam disobeyed and brought shame and death upon himself and his descendants, but the last man Adam obeyed and brought life and immortality to all mankind; to all who choose to believe.

The second man Jesus Christ overcame evil by choosing the Father's will over His own will. And so complete and satisfying was His Calvary sacrifice that He has become not only the redeemer of Adam's fallen race but the governor of God's universe as predetermined.

Satan contrived Adam's fall and became the possessor of the power of death and is called "the prince of the authority of the air." Through the power of death through sin, Satan gained control over Adam and his descendants. But, this power and authority Satan possesses is forever broken by Jesus Christ.

As our great high priest, Jesus Christ offered up a perfect sacrifice of His own unblemished life for all mankind. This is the meaning of His resurrection statement: "All power is given unto me in heaven and in earth" (Mathew 28:18b). Jesus offered to God a perfect and better sacrifice than that of the Levitical priesthood of Aaron and Moses with their sacrifices of goat and bulls:

> "But Christ being come an high priest of good things to come, by a greater and more perfect tabernacle, not made with hands, that is to say, not of this building. Neither by the blood of goats and calves, but by his own blood he entered in once into the holy place, having obtained eternal redemption for us" (Hebrews 9:11-12).

The Aaronic priesthood and sacrifices were deficient and imperfect; therefore, it had to be repeated every year. But, this is not the case with the one time sacrifice of Christ which was done through the eternal Spirit. His sacrifice was better, sufficient and complete for all people of every generation. Never to be repeated:

> "For if the blood of bulls and of goats, and the ashes of an heifer sprinkling the unclean, sanctifieth to the purifying of the flesh: How much more shall the blood of Christ, who through the eternal Spirit offered himself without spot to God, purge your conscience from dead works to serve the living God?
>
> And for this cause he is the mediator of the new testament, that by means of death, for the redemption of the transgressions that were under the first testament, they which are called might receive the promise of eternal inheritance" (Hebrews 9:13-15)

No more sacrifice is required or needed for the expiation of man's sins. God is satisfied with what He has done through the Son would not accept any other oblation or sacrifice. In Him, all human sacrifices and libations comes to an end, they cease.

Jesus Christ is the end of the law and it does not matter whose law. Far from setting the law aside, He vindicates the law:

Chapter 4: Why God Became a Man

"For the law having a shadow of good things to come, and not the very image of the things, can never with those sacrifices which they offered year by year continually make the comers thereunto perfect.

For then would they not have ceased to be offered? Because that the worshippers once purged should have had no more conscience of sins. But in those sacrifices there is a remembrance again made of sins every year" (Hebrews 10:1-3).

Again, the high priesthood of Jesus Christ is superior to that of the Aaronic priesthood and is compared to that of Melchizedek King of Salem (Genesis 14:18). God testified of Jesus Christ saying: "Thou art a priest forever after the order of Melchisedec" (Hebrews 7:17):

"As he saith also in another place, Thou art a priest for ever after the order of Melchisedec. Who in the days of his flesh, when he had offered up prayers and supplications with strong crying and tears unto him that was able to save him from death, and was heard in that he feared.

Though he were a Son, yet learned he obedience by the things which he suffered. And being made perfect, he became the author of eternal salvation unto all them that obey him. Called of God an high priest after the order of Melchisedec" (Hebrews 5:6-10; cf. chapters 6 & 7)

Abraham gave Melchizedek a tenth part of all his spoils (tithe) because, as priest of the Most High God, He was God's representative. Abraham (the less) was blessed by Melchizedek (the greater, cf. Hebrews 7:7).

All creation is called upon to worship and be blessed by so doing. Jesus Christ, who is made not after the law of carnal commandment, but after the power of endless life with an unchangeable priesthood is the surety of a better testament. A silent warning to all men is this:

"Kiss the Son, lest he be angry, and ye perish from the way, when his wrath is kindled but a little. Blessed are all they that put their trust in him" (Psalm 2:12).

By His vicarious and expiation sacrifice, Jesus Christ the Son of God has abolished death for you and me. Death in all of its stages and forms are abolished forever for all who choose to believe the Gospel of Jesus Christ.

Through Christ sin is undone and forgiven, death ends in resurrection, sinners become saints and the works of Satan is destroyed forever:

"But is now made manifest by the appearing of our Saviour Jesus Christ, who hath abolished death, and hath brought life and immortality to light through the gospel" (2 Timothy 1:10; Hebrews 2:14).

Spiritual death, which Adam experienced immediately after he ate of the forbidden fruit, and of which all born from him experience, including newly born babies and children who have not committed any known sin, was done away by the death and resurrection of the Son of God (Romans 5:14; Ephesians 2:1-8).

The keys of death and hell are no longer in Satan's hands; they are firmly in the hands of Jesus Christ our Savior and substitute:

"Fear not; I am the first and the last: I am he that liveth, and was dead; and, behold, I am alive forevermore, Amen; and has the keys of hell and of death" (Revelation 1:18).

Any man who believes in Jesus Christ can be saved from death. Yes, we may all suffer physical death, but we shall not all experience eternal death. This is what Jesus said to Martha when her brother Lazarus died:

"Jesus said unto her, I am the resurrection, and the life: he that believeth in me, though he were dead, yet shall

Chapter 4: Why God Became a Man

he live. And whosoever liveth and believeth in me shall never die. Believest thou this?" (John 11:25-26).

Further, any one who puts his or her faith in God through Jesus Christ would not experience the punishment of eternal death (the lake of fire). God declares all believers and would absolutely acquit them on the Day of Judgment.

Hell is only for those who reject God's righteousness. Heaven is the home of all who choose to believe the Gospel of salvation instead of their own works or efforts (Revelation 20:10-15; 21:8).

There cannot be fellowship with God where sin is not dealt with. "God is light, and in Him is no darkness at all." If it were not for the atoning death of Jesus Christ fellowship with God for fallen man would never have been possible.

It is the blood of Jesus that cleanses us from all sin when we confess and forsake them (cf. 1 John 1:9-10). At the moment, Jesus Christ is the believer's attorney in heaven. If we sin we are in trouble with the Father, but Jesus stands before the Father on our behalf (cf. 1 John 2:1-2).

Below is how Jesus Christ, the last Adam compares with first man Adam:

> **"Wherefore, as by one man sin entered into the world, and death by sin; and so death passed upon all men, for that all have sinned: (For until the law sin was in the world: but sin is not imputed when there is no law.**
>
> **Nevertheless death reigned from Adam to Moses, even over them that had not sinned after the similitude of Adam's transgression, who is the figure of him that was to come.**
>
> **But not as the offence, so also is the free gift. For if through the offence of one many be dead, much more the grace of God, and the gift by grace, which is by one man, Jesus Christ, hath abounded unto many. And not as it**

was by one that sinned, so is the gift: for the judgment was by one to condemnation, but the free gift is of many offences unto justification.

For if by one man's offence death reigned by one; much more they which receive abundance of grace and of the gift of righteousness shall reign in life by one, Jesus Christ). Therefore as by the offence of one judgment came upon all men to condemnation; even so by the righteousness of one the free gift came upon all men unto justification of life.

For as by one man's disobedience many were made sinners, so by the obedience of one shall many be made righteous. Moreover the law entered, that the offence might abound.

But where sin abounded, grace did much more abound: That as sin hath reigned unto death, even so might grace reign through righteousness unto eternal life by Jesus Christ our Lord" (Romans 5:12-21).

The effect of the sacrifice of the second man Jesus Christ is far greater than the damage done through the sin from first man Adam. For example, it was not the lifetime sins of Adam that brought death to the whole of mankind, but the one time original sin.

On the contrary, the one time sacrifice of the sinless and obedient Son of God provides total cleansing from all sins throughout eternity. Amen! All men must come to Jesus Christ for salvation if all men are to be saved.

The two men, Adam and Jesus Christ, determine the final destination of every man. I have a few contrasts here to help clarify where these two men stand as far as the salvation of the human race is concerned:

	First man Adam (old humanity)	Last man Jesus Christ (new humanity)
1.	Of the Earth	Lord of heaven
2.	Living soul	Life giving Spirit
3.	Disobedient	Obedient
4.	Brought sin	Brought righteousness
5.	Brought condemnation	Brought Justification
6.	Offence brought death	Obedience brought life
7.	Sin brought in the law	Righteousness brought in grace
8.	By one man sin, many are dead	By one man's righteousness, many are made righteous.
9.	Sinners get what they deserve	Sinners get what they do not deserve
10.	Sin is imputed	Righteousness is imputed
11.	All die	All are made alive
12.	Head of the human race	Head of the new man
13.	Representative of created humanity	Representative of new spiritual humanity
14.	Reigns in death	Reigns in life
15.	Brought curse	Brought blessing
16.	Separation from God	Reconciled to God
17.	Judgment	Justification
18.	Sinned for every man	Died for every man
19.	Brought strife	Brought peace

You can also read these references for additional blessing (cf. Romans 5:12-21; 1 Corinthians 15:45-48; 2 Corinthians 5:11ff).

Now, you see why Jesus Christ is irreplaceable. Because of sin in the nature of every man, we must all be born again to enter the kingdom of God. In Adam we all die, but in Jesus Christ we all can live.

It is absolutely impossible for God to die, but for the love wherein God loved us, He voluntarily became a man and tasted death for every man including you and me (2 Corinthians 5). As the incarnate Son, Jesus suffered our pain, shame, guilt, afflictions and died on behalf of all men:

> "Seeing then that we have a great high priest, that is passed into the heavens, Jesus the Son of God, let us hold fast our profession. For we have not an high priest which cannot be touched with the feeling of our infirmities; but was in all points tempted like as we are, yet without sin" (Hebrews 4:14-15).

Man has broken a divine law and is punishable by death and the only remedy is the death of the righteous Son of God. Each and every man is forever lost without Jesus Christ. He came into the world to seek and to save His human creatures:

> "For the Son of man is come to seek and to save that which was lost" (Luke 19:10).

Through death, He took away the sins and the punishment for sin; He took away the wrath of God. The testimony of the Bible is that, God so loved the world that He gave His one and only Son to die for every man so that we may live through Him. Now, heaven or hell is up to each of us to decide:

> "For God so loved the world that he gave his one and only Son, that whoever believes in him shall not perish but have eternal life. For God did not send his Son into the world to condemn the world, but to save the world through him.
>
> Whoever believes in him is not condemned, but whoever does not believe stands condemned already because he has not believed in the name of God's one and only Son" (John 3:16-18).

> "God sent not his Son into the world to condemn the world; but that the world through him might be saved" (John

3:17). Jesus did not come to judge the world, but to save the world" (John 12:47). However, when He comes the second time He would surely judge the world. But, for now, God has appointed and anointed His Son to bring salvation to all who would express the need and reach out for it:

> "Behold my servant, whom I uphold; mine elect, in whom my soul delighteth; I have put my spirit upon him: he shall bring forth judgment to the Gentiles" (Isaiah 42:1).

To date, all the self-efforts of man to find God and to please Him have never been cheap and easy. It has been very painful, costly and vain. In Scripture, God speaks to man saying: "Stand ye in the ways, and see, and ask for the old paths, where is the good way, and walk therein, and ye shall find rest for your souls" (Jeremiah 6:16).

In another place God speaks to all saying:

> "I love them that love me; and those that seek me early shall find me" (Proverbs 8:17):

Chapter three of Genesis to the last chapter of the book of Revelation is all about the restoration of man from the fall. If not for the fall, there would have being no need for God to become a man and die such a painful death for us. Also, there would have being no need for prisons, hospitals, war, divorce, idolatry and all other forms of wickedness and unrighteousness of men.

But, the good news is that, man would not be lost forever. There is a second chance for every man in Jesus Christ. The will of God for every man is to be saved (Genesis 3; 2 Timothy 1:2). Let every man stop wasting time and self-efforts to please God or to establish a right relationship with Him.

Mere praying, fasting and pleading with God through the dead only serve to worsen things. They serve no purpose. God would not and has not forgotten man whom He has created in His own likeness and image. His mercies are renewed every morning. Truth is the very essence of the Gospel:

"For this is good and acceptable in the sight of God our Saviour; who will have all men to be saved, and to come unto the knowledge of the truth" (1 Timothy 2: 3-4).

Even though creation was a one time event, the fall of man has kept Him working from the day He rested. For the love wherein He loved mankind God became a man to help us. God is great in kindness and mercy.

As God, Jesus represents God. As a man, He represents man before God.

"There is one God and one mediator between God and men, the man Christ Jesus" (1 Timothy 2: 5).

Here is my conclusion for this chapter. Adam's original sin is man's sin and Christ's one act of obedience can be man's righteousness. Soberly reflect and meditate on this quotation as you prepare for the next chapter:

"And without controversy great is the mystery of godliness: God was manifest in the flesh, justified in the Spirit, seen of angels, preached unto the Gentiles, believed on in the world, received up into glory" (1 Timothy 3:16).

Now, relax and get ready to launch into the deep. If there are places in God's word where babies can swim, there are places where giants can also swim. Where God ends is where man begins. This chapter completes our foundation on the person of Christ.

Chapter 5

JESUS CHRIST AND CREATION

Jesus Christ is before all things. He was at the beginning of creation and took part in the creation of our universe. The beginning means the beginning of everything but God – the beginning of nature and man:

"And he is before all things, and by him all things consist" (Colossians 1:17).

Jesus Christ was the Word by whom all things were made. Dominions, thrones, principalities, visible and invisible were created by Him. He is the reason for man's existence: "All things were made by him; and without him was not any thing made that was made" (John 1:3):

"For by him were all things created, that are in heaven, and that are in earth, visible and invisible, whether they be thrones, or dominions, or principalities, or powers: all things were created by him, and for him: And he is before all things, and by him all things consist" (Colossians 1:16-17).

As you can see from the above quotations the universe has not always existed. God made the universe for His only Son Jesus Christ and conditioned the heaven and the earth as a home for human beings:

"The heaven, even the heavens, are the LORD's: but the earth hath he given to the children of men" (Psalm 115:16).

According to the word of God, Jesus Christ is the Creator, not the created. He is the subject and not the object of creation:

"And to make all men see what is the fellowship of the mystery, which from the beginning of the world hath been hid in God, who created all things by Jesus Christ" (Ephesians 3:9).

He, through whom all things were made and preserved, must of necessity be before the beginning. We are His offspring: "For in him we live, and move, and have our being" (Acts 17:28).

Genesis chapters one and two provide humanity with two simple, logical and unsophisticated accounts of creation. According to the Bible, God created all things by His Word. He simply called creation into being by His Word and by His Spirit:

"By the word of the LORD were the heavens made; and all the host of them by the breath of his mouth" (Psalm 33:6).

There is no declaration of date for the beginning. The Bible does not explain the existence of God; it assumes His existence. Unless we want to fill in the blanks as we always try to do, the divine testimony, as narrated in the Bible, is adequate for the finite mind. God gave us what we need.

The Biblical account of creation is not scientific and must be accepted only by faith. "Faith is the substance of things hoped for, the evidence of things not seen."

"Through faith we understand that the worlds were framed by the word of God, so that things which are seen were not made of things which do appear" (Hebrews 11:3; cf. Psalm 33:6).

Chapter 5: Jesus Christ and Creation

Man did not evolve. Man is not nature's mistake. Man was purposely created by God. God created the first adult male and the first adult female. The name Adam, given to first man, emphasizes man's createdness:

"And the LORD God formed man of the dust of the ground, and breathed into his nostrils the breath of life; and man became a living soul" (Genesis 2:7).

Adam is said to be a figure (type) of Him (Jesus Christ) that is to come. He is the only Old Testament character to be called explicitly a type of Christ. Adam was created in Christ Jesus unto good works (cf. Ephesians 2:10).

If we want to know the degree and quality of life and lifestyle man was originally made of, we can take a look at Jesus Christ. God did not make man the way he is; man is what he is today because of his own sin. Man fits himself for destruction. God never does that

Jesus is both the life and the light of men. Life is in Him and from Him. Likewise, light is in Him and from Him. Both natural and spiritual life emanates in Him and from Him:

"In him was life; and the life was the light of men" (John 1:4).

God is the source of all knowledge. He is the source of all the facts that are observed and classified as science. I believe Science would be plain common sense if only man can accept the plain testimony of the Bible because it is an eye witness account.

God created both natural and spiritual laws, the visible and the invisible world. As the Sovereign Lord, He makes the rules and man and angels obey. As the only Law-Maker, He is free to alter, interpose or even work outside His laws.

Personally, I do not think science can be separated from faith. Like the coin with two sides, the spiritual is the other side of the natural. Natural science and faith must go hand in hand. After all, man is not just matter. He is both matter and spirit.

Doctors must feel free and not hesitate to recommend faith healing to their incurably diseased patients. God made the herbs and trees from which we get our medicines through the agency of His Word.

God is free to choose the means to heal the human body, soul, and spirit. God can directly heal us by His word (Word) or through nature. Here is what the psalmist has to say concerning healing:

"He sent his word, and healed them, and delivered them from their destructions" (Psalm 107:20).

God has provided humanity with both natural and Spiritual healing. By Spiritual healing, I mean healings through the Holy Spirit and not that of fetish and pseudo-prophets. God sent Jesus Christ, the eternal Word, to heal mankind. The word of God is for our healing and nourishment.

Jesus Christ is the true bread from heaven that gives life to the world. He is the ransom and the receipt that God has fully paid for all human diseases both physical and spiritual:

"It is written, Man shall not live by bread alone, but by every word that proceedeth out of the mouth of God" (Mathew 4:4; cf. 8:16; John 6:32-33; Isaiah 53).

The secular can be better understood through the sacred. That which is invisible can be understood from the visible. Faith fills the vacuum and answers the unanswerable in natural science. Faith is the gateway to the supernatural:

"For the invisible things of him from the creation of the world are clearly seen, being understood by the things that are made" (Romans 1:20a).

Our existence is directly connected to our understanding of both spiritual and natural life. Our Creator lives and communicates with us from the invisible realm through Jesus and the invisible Holy Spirit. A misunderstanding of either of the two realms is fatal to our very existence here and hereafter.

Chapter 5: Jesus Christ and Creation

The truth that God made the world and man by Jesus Christ and by Him they exist can only be received by faith. It is a fact, that we turn to disbelief what we do not understand or see. We pick and choose what we want to belief.

But, here is the truth: "Without faith in Jesus Christ it is impossible to know the One and only true God." He is the only access to our invisible Creator. In summary, Jesus Christ is the Creator and the reason for creation.

Notes

Chapter 6

THE SEED OF THE WOMAN

Now, tread carefully because the ground you are approaching is holy and perhaps demands that you take off your shoes (Exodus 3:5).

The first announcement of the coming Savior-Messiah Jesus Christ came immediately after the fall of man nearly six thousand years ago. The period when man lived in innocence (without sin) was relatively short.

God announced in the form of promise that the seed of the woman shall destroy the works of Satan. The Son of God who shall be born of a woman without a human father shall destroy sin or the works of the devil forever.

The seed of the woman shall disarm the powers of darkness and openly put them to shame. He would overcome them by His sinless life, death and victorious resurrection (Colossians 2:15):

> "And I will put enmity between thee and the woman, and between thy seed and her seed; it shall bruise thy head, and thou shalt bruise his heel" (Genesis 3:15).

Isaiah, speaking almost seven hundred years later, revealed the identity of this woman as a virgin – an unmarried woman of marriageable age.

According to the Scriptures, before this woman knows

a man or engages in any sexual act, she shall be found with a child and shall give birth to a son whose name is to be called "Emmanuel," a name which means, "God with us". This title describes the deity of the person of the Son of God:

> "Therefore the Lord himself shall give you a sign; Behold, a virgin shall conceive, and bear a son, and shall call his name Immanuel" (Isaiah 7:14).

Today, both prophecies have been fulfilled. At the time appointed by the Father, and as foretold by the prophets, a woman called Mary, a virgin and wife to a man called Joseph a carpenter by trade, gave birth to a son who bore the double name Jesus Christ in history:

> "But when the fullness of the time was come, God sent forth his Son, made of a woman, made under the law" (Galatians 4:4).

According to the Scriptures, before Mary and Joseph were officially joined as husband and wife, and before there was any sexual intercourse between them, Mary was found to be with a child (pregnant).

The Jewish culture in those days required one year of betrothal before the bride could take residence in the home of the groom and consummate the marriage. It was during this interval that Virgin Mary miraculously was conceived by the Holy Ghost (Spirit).

Here is the Bible's own testimony concerning the birth of Jesus Christ the Son of God from both the Gospel according to Mathew and Luke:

> "Now the birth of Jesus Christ was on this wise: When as his mother Mary was espoused to Joseph, before they came together, she was found with child of the Holy Ghost. Then Joseph her husband, being a just man, and not willing to make her a public example, was minded to put her away privily.

But while he thought on these things, behold, the angel of the LORD appeared unto him in a dream, saying, Joseph, thou son of David, fear not to take unto thee Mary thy wife: for that which is conceived in her is of the Holy Ghost.

And she shall bring forth a son, and thou shalt call his name JESUS: for he shall save his people from their sins. Now all this was done, that it might be fulfilled which was spoken of the Lord by the prophet, saying,

Behold, a virgin shall be with child, and shall bring forth a son, and they shall call his name Emmanuel, which being interpreted is, God with us.

Then Joseph being raised from sleep did as the angel of the Lord had bidden him, and took unto him his wife: And knew her not till she had brought forth her firstborn son: and he called his name JESUS" (Mathew 1:18-25).

"And, behold, thou shalt conceive in thy womb, and bring forth a son, and shalt call his name JESUS.

He shall be great, and shall be called the Son of the Highest: and the Lord God shall give unto him the throne of his father David:

And he shall reign over the house of Jacob for ever; and of his kingdom there shall be no end.

Then said Mary unto the angel, How shall this be, seeing I know not a man?

And the angel answered and said unto her, The Holy Ghost shall come upon thee, and the power of the Highest shall overshadow thee: therefore also that holy thing which shall be born of thee shall be called the Son of God.

And, behold, thy cousin Elisabeth, she hath also conceived a son in her old age: and this is the sixth month with her, who was called barren.

For with God nothing shall be impossible. And Mary said, Behold the handmaid of the Lord; be it unto me according to thy word. And the angel departed from her" (Luke 1:31-38).

Apart from Jesus Christ, no man alive or dead has fully fulfilled the divine requirement as set forth in the Holy Scriptures. No man has ever been born without a human father. The birth of Jesus Christ was a miracle of all miracles.

Virgin Mary gave birth to a Son without the help of a man two thousand years ago. If the human zygote typically has 46 chromosomes in total (twenty three from each of the parent) as science tells us, then it was utterly impossible and may be a stretch of imagination for Mary alone with twenty three chromosomes to give birth to a full human being.

The question may be, did God take 23 chromosomes from Mary and twenty three from Himself to fuse together to make baby Jesus? The answer is, absolutely not. Further, did God have sexual intercourse with Mary? And the answer is blasphemy.

God provided all the 46 chromosomes needed to make Jesus Christ fully man. The Creator of the universe is the Father of Jesus Christ (cf. Luke 2:41-49). Mary herself indicated that: "With God all things are possible."

God the Holy Spirit created a body for the Son of God in the womb of Mary. He made an earthly body for the Eternal Word to cloth Himself with full humanity: "The Word was made Flesh" in the womb of Virgin Mary (cf. John 1:14):

"Wherefore when he cometh into the world, he saith, Sacrifice and offering thou wouldest not, but a body hast thou prepared me" (Hebrews 10:5).

Jesus clothing Himself with humanity does not mean He ceased to be God. He was fully God all the time He was fully man, but chose not to exercise His privileges as God as already mentioned. He came to earth full of truth and grace and the dispenser of both to all who choose to believe.

Jesus Christ possessed the glory no man has or would ever have, but chose to humble Himself as the servant of all men. Jesus Christ is the unique One; the only kind the world has ever known and would ever know:

"And we beheld his glory, the glory as of the only begotten of the Father, full of grace and truth" (John 1:14).

Further, as God, Jesus Christ did not enter a human body or join Himself to man – He became fully man. This is what the apostle Paul called the "mystery of Godliness:"

"And without controversy great is the mystery of godliness: God was manifest in the flesh, justified in the Spirit, seen of angels, preached unto the Gentiles, believed on in the world, received up into glory" (1 Timothy 3:16).

Jesus Christ did not only take on a human body, He took to Himself also our human nature. In the incarnation, the Son of God added to His divine nature our human nature. The human nature was not absorbed or fused into the divine; no, that was not the case. While He was still divine, He became human.

The Eternal Word became what He was not in the incarnation – a man. Jesus Christ, in the incarnation, was a man as if He was no God and God as if He was no man.

The seed of the woman came from heaven with His name (Genesis 3:15). Joseph, the legal but not the human father of Jesus Christ, was instructed by the messenger from heaven to call the first born son of Mary, Jesus:

"Thou shalt call His name Jesus for He shall save His people from their sins."

Only God can save man from sin and death, and this is exactly what Jesus Christ came to do for all men. The Lord and Savior of the Old Testament is Jesus the Savior of the New Testament if you can take it:

> "Ye are my witnesses, saith the LORD, and my servant whom I have chosen: that ye may know and believe me, and understand that I am he: before me there was no God formed, neither shall there be after me.
>
> I, even I, am the LORD; and beside me there is no saviour. I have declared, and have saved, and I have shewed, when there was no strange god among you: therefore ye are my witnesses, saith the LORD, that I am God" (Isaiah 43:10-12).

"All the promises of God in Christ are yea, and in him amen" (Romans 15:8). Has God made any promise to you or given you a vision of some sort? Please, wait for it, for it shall surely come to pass:

> "For the vision is yet for an appointed time . . . and not lie: though it tarries, wait for it; because it will surely come" (2 Corinthians 1:20; Habakkuk 2:3).

Whatever took place in Mary's womb was a divine conception. It was against the natural order of things. Jesus was born a full human being without the handed down sinful nature from Adam through Mary.

But, how could this be? Since the Bible says, no man can bring a clean thing out of the unclean (cf. Job 14:4; 15:14). Again, the Scripture says "what is man, that he could be pure? And he who is born of a woman, that he could be righteous? (Job 15:14).

The answer to these questions and Jesus' mysterious and unique pregnancy is God. Here is the process:

> **"The Holy Ghost shall come upon thee, and the power of the highest shall overshadow thee: therefore also that holy thing which shall be born of thee shall be called the Son of God"** (Luke 1:35).

When Mary asked the messenger from heaven "How shall this be, seeing I know not a man? The angel answered, the Holy

Chapter 6: The Seed of the Woman

Ghost shall do it. He shall brood over you and that "holy thing" shall be born.

The Holy Spirit shall overshadow you and He shall cause the holy thing, meaning Jesus, to be born. Notice that the angel or the messenger from heaven refrained from using the word baby: "Therefore also that holy thing which shall be born of thee shall be called the Son of God."

Jesus was made like us in every way but without sin or any diminishing in His human nature. God brought a clean baby out of that which was tainted with sin (Luke 1:47; cf. Philippians 3:21). Remember, with God all things are possible.

Mary herself admitted that it was by the grace of God that she has been chosen. She recognized her own sinfulness in her humility (Luke 1:48; cf. Philippians 3:21; James 1:10). "In sin did my mother conceive me," is true for every human including Mary; so, for her to give birth to a baby without sin was a stupendous act of God (Psalm 51:5; cf. Job 14:4).

Again, Jesus was not only born without sin, but He lived His entire life in this sin-filled and sin-plagued world without sin. So far, He is the only man ever to come out of the lineage of Adam to live and die without sin. He did no sin, neither was any guile ever found in His mouth:

> **"Who did no sin, neither was guile found in his mouth: Who, when he was reviled, reviled not again; when he suffered, he threatened not; but committed himself to him that judgeth righteously" (1 Peter 2:22-23).**

Perhaps another question you may want to ask at this stage is: Does not Jesus Christ sinlessness alone apart from anything else extol Him above all men and qualify Him to be the Savior of sinners as indicated by the Bible? Certainly it does. Otherwise, how can a sinner save a fellow sinner? Only He that is free from sin can free those who are held hostage by it (Romans 5:12)? Jesus Christ is a man, but separate from sinners:

"For such an high priest became us, who is holy, harmless, undefiled, separate from sinners, and made higher than the heavens" (Hebrews 7:26).

Further, someone may also say, Jesus Christ is a god or God and that is why He was able to live without sin and wrought such stupendous miracles. Again, this is far from the truth. Mary's baby was a human baby. He was made of the seed of David according to the flesh (cf. Romans 1:3; 2 Samuel 7:13).

Remember, Jesus Christ did not enter the world as God. He came as a man and was born as man and lived His entire life as a man and died as a man. Jesus Christ came into this world as the "Representative man" – to represent all men.

There was no obscurity in His deity and neither was there any obtruding in His manhood:

"Wherefore in all things it behooved him to be made like unto his brethren, that he might be a merciful and faithful high priest in things pertaining to God, to make reconciliation for the sins of the sins of the people (Hebrews 2:17; cf. verse 14).

The Redeemer and Savior of the human race had a body that was made of the same material as the people He had come to save. Jesus was born subject to the ordinary laws of human development. His body and mental life were both represented as having undergone a natural development (cf. Mathew 2:2; 4:2; Luke 1; 2; John 4:6; 11:35; 12:27; Hebrews 2:10,18; 5:7,8).

Every one professing to be under the influence of the Spirit of God cannot deny that Jesus Christ was a man. He cannot deny that there was real incarnation. He did not come in appearance only and neither did He merely seem to be a man, and to suffer and die. Jesus the Christ in the incarnation was 100% man.

Unfortunately, there are many who carry such erroneous view about His manhood, being deceived themselves and deceiving others:

Chapter 6: The Seed of the Woman

"For many deceivers are entered into the world, who confess not that Jesus Christ is come in the flesh. This is a deceiver and an antichrist" (2 John 1:7).

To say that "Jesus Christ is not come in the flesh" is dangerous, because it is a denial of the reality of the work of redemption accomplished through Him for all mankind. Further, it renders the whole plan of Salvation a lie.

Furthermore, Jesus Christ pre-resurrection body was not a spiritual body. It was of the same material you, I and everybody alive are made of. Not withstanding, be aware His post-resurrection body was of a different quality:

"And every spirit that confesseth not that Jesus Christ is come in the flesh is not of God: and this is that spirit of antichrist, whereof ye have heard that it should come; and even now already is it in the world" (1 John 4:3).

We have Jesus pre-natal and post natal records with us today. He was breast fed, carried in the arms of His mother just like any baby, protected by His parents, circumcised, dedicated in the temple, baptized at the age of thirty, and had siblings.

For example, when the witnessing soldier at the cross of His crucifixion pierced His side with a spear, what came out from the wound was blood and water:

But one of the soldiers with a spear pierced his side, and forthwith came there out blood and water" (John 19:34).

Please, do not buy into all the myths concerning His person. Again, here is my warning, "if it is not in the Bible, it is not worth knowing." "God never leaves lose ends." Lest I forget and conclude this important chapter, I would like to pay my respect to "Mary," the mother of Jesus Christ.

Truly, I applaud the fact that the church of Jesus Christ is grateful to this young lady who at such tender age accepted the message from the angel even though it was beyond her wildest imagination by confessing, "Be it unto me according to thy Word." Her faith is highly recommendable.

In the same vein, let me also take a moment to plead with my beloved brethren of the faith to be careful not to fall into the trap of being rendered "blasphemy and idolaters" for calling and worshiping Mary as the "mother of God." To place Mary between the sinner and the eternal Son of God is a deviation from Scripture.

Mary is the mother of the incarnate Son of God (the promised seed of David) – she is the honored mother of the most powerful and influential man in the universe and I do not think we or any being can in any way confer a greater honor to her than that which is already accorded to her by God.

Further, ask yourself, how Mary can call God, "My Savior, if God was her Son? (cf. Luke 1:47). Mary is dead, but Jesus Christ who after His resurrection was declared "Lord" lives on. He is alive and well.

Further still, as to the issue of "her immaculate conception (conception without sin)," the question we may all ask is, by what means and at what point did Mary become sinless (without sin). The cardinal teaching of the Scriptures concerning fallen humanity is that "without the shedding of blood (the blood of the incarnate Son) there is no remission of sin."

God crowned Jesus Christ with great honor and glory as Lord and Christ by the Spirit of holiness, by the resurrection from the dead to save all men including Mary:

> **"Therefore let all the house of Israel know assuredly, that God hath made the same Jesus, whom ye have crucified, both Lord and Christ" (Acts 2:36; 10:36; Romans 1:4; Hebrew 1; Revelation 4 and 5).**

Again, be aware that, Jesus Christ coming into the earth as a man and being born as a man (His humiliation) was not honored as "Lord' until His victory over sin, Satan and death (His exaltation):

> **"Thou hast loved righteousness, and hated iniquity; therefore God, even thy God, hath anointed thee with the oil of gladness above thy fellows" (Hebrews 1:9; cf. Daniel 7:13-14; Philippians 2:7).**

His Place of Birth

The prophet Micah prophesied of His place of birth centuries before Jesus was born as Bethlehem of Judea which is also called Ephratah. This Judean city was the birth place of David and also the original city of Joseph's ancestors:

> "But thou, Bethlehem Ephratah, though thou be little among the thousands of Judah, yet out of thee shall he come forth unto me that is to be ruler in Israel; whose goings forth have been from of old, from everlasting" (Micah 5:2).

The "ruler in Israel" who would come from Bethlehem is none other than the child-ruler predicted by the prophet Isaiah: "For unto us a child is born, unto us a son is given; and the government shall be upon his shoulder" (Isaiah 9:6). According to Scripture, this "ruler" is also the "mighty God."

According to the Biblical account, around the time of His birth, Joseph had to travel with Mary from Nazareth to Bethlehem for the census and Jesus was born in a stable during their time in Bethlehem in fulfillment of Micah's prophecy. Here is the Biblical narration:

> "And Joseph also went up from Galilee, out of the city of Nazareth, into Judaea, unto the city of David, which is called Bethlehem; (because he was of the house and lineage of David).
>
> To be taxed with Mary his espoused wife, being great with child. And so it was, that, while they were there, the days were accomplished that she should be delivered.
>
> And she brought forth her firstborn son, and wrapped him in swaddling clothes, and laid him in a manger; because there was no room for them in the inn" (Luke 2:3-7; cf. Mathew 2:1).

Jesus Christ is the fulfillment of the prophecies of both Isaiah and Micah.

Time of His Birth

As to the time of Jesus birth, Luke tells us that John the Baptist began his public ministry in the fifteenth year of Tiberius Caesar. Jesus was baptized by John the same year.

According to some historians the reign of Tiberius began 19th August, A.D. 14, so the fifteenth year when Jesus Christ commenced His public ministry was A.D. 29:

"In the fifteenth year of the reign of Tiberius Caesar— when Pontius Pilate was governor of Judea, Herod tetrarch of Galilee, his brother Philip tetrarch of Iturea and Traconitis, and Lysanias tetrarch of Abilene" (Luke 3:1).

The first Passover of our Lord's ministry took place the same year; three Passovers after A. D. 32, He was crucified. There seems to be no consensus among historians and theologians as to the exact date of our Lord's birth but the majority put His date of birth between 4 B.C. and 7 A. D.

I guess the issue here is not the exactness of His date of birth, but the fact that He was born to this earth.

We should be able to separate the essential from the important. Here the essential is that, Jesus Christ the Son of God was indeed a natural citizen of this earth. You can also calculate to a greater degree of accuracy from the prophet Daniel's "Seventy Weeks," His date of birth (cf. Daniel 9:20ff).

His Growing Up

There is no mention of His size, color of hair, eyes and no age classification and even education. Suffice to say, the Bible is profoundly disinterested in Jesus Christ physical appearance. Man looks on the outward but God looks inward.

We are what we are in the mind and heart and not the color

of our skin. However, I can tell you this; He is nothing like what we have in our homes and church buildings. All the works of sculptors and painters about him are mere works of fantasy.

True, He was a Palestinian Jew and definitely looked and dressed like one. True, He probably spoke both Aramaic and Greek and maybe Latin. But, the closest description anyone can get is that which is provided by the prophet Isaiah given centuries before He was born:

"Who hath believed our report? and to whom is the arm of the LORD revealed? For he shall grow up before him as a tender plant, and as a root out of a dry ground: he hath no form nor comeliness; and when we shall see him, there is no beauty that we should desire him" (Isaiah 53:1-2).

Jesus grew up a normal human being; passing through all the stages of psychological development: infancy, childhood, adolescence, and manhood. There was nothing grotesque or abnormal about His growth from adult to manhood. He grew and developed healthy and normal:

"And the child grew, and waxed strong in spirit, filled with wisdom: and the grace of God was upon him" (Luke 2:40).

Jesus Christ could read and write (Luke 4:17; John 8:6-8), probably leaving school around the age of fifteen as it may be the case of any Jewish boy.

At the age of twelve He was thought to be missing only to be found three days after in the temple having discussions with the doctors (Luke 2:42-49).

He followed the trade of His legal father Joseph and became a carpenter (Mark 6:3). He had siblings (Mark 3:31).

Here is another admonition - beware of all the fanciful and fictitious legends about the silent years. We can always detect the source of a particular religion whether it is of God or Satan by what they say about Jesus Christ.

For example, if someone knocks on your door to tell you about God, first ask what he or she thinks of Jesus Christ. If the answer does not subscribe to that of the Bible then you should be the one doing all the talking.

Jesus Christ is not a mystical figure or the spiritual man that many claim Him to be. Here is a strong warning from the Scriptures:

> "Beloved, believe not every spirit, but try the spirits whether they are of God: because many false prophets are gone out into the world.
>
> Hereby know ye the Spirit of God: Every spirit that confesseth that Jesus Christ is come in the flesh is of God:
>
> And every spirit that confesseth not that Jesus Christ is come in the flesh is not of God: and this is that spirit of antichrist, whereof ye have heard that it should come; and even now already is it in the world" (1 John 4:2-3).

All heresies major in denial of Jesus Christ as revealed in Scripture:

> "For many deceivers are entered into the world, who confess not that Jesus Christ is come in the flesh. This is a deceiver and an antichrist" (2 John 1:7).

As a man Jesus lived, worked, and was subject to all the weaknesses, trials, and temptation peculiar to all men. He depended on God for His sustenance, protection and help. He was obedient to the will of God only through the power of the Holy Spirit (Mathew 26:39; John 4:34; 18).

Though he was the Son of God, he learned obedience by the things which he suffered as a man. He felt every human emotion, asked questions to elicit information and made prayer a lifestyle. He prayed earnestly, sometimes with tears.

He expressed surprises and probably suffered more physical pain than any human being:

"Who in the days of his flesh, when he had offered up prayers and supplications with strong crying and tears unto him that was able to save him from death, and was heard in that he feared.

Though he were a Son, yet learned he obedience by the things which he suffered. And being made perfect, he became the author of eternal salvation unto all them that obey him" (Hebrews 5:7-9).

The Manner of man

The angel Gabriel, the messenger from heaven gave the information on the manner of man the son of Mary would be saying:

"He shall be great, and shall be called the Son of the highest: and the Lord shall give unto him the throne of his father David. He shall reign over the house of Jacob (Israel) forever; and of his kingdom there shall be no end" (Luke 1:32-33).

And truly this is exactly how we know Jesus Christ on earth. He is indeed a great man but His present greatness as we know Him to be now cannot and will not in any way be compared to His glory when He returns to earth.

Jesus Christ was a man of impeccable character; He was not violent, never cursed back or paid evil with evil. In fact, let me save you the trouble of an endless list of His holiness in life and service by quoting from the Bible:

"For even hereunto were ye called: because Christ also suffered for us, leaving us an example, that ye should follow his steps: Who did no sin, neither was guile found in his mouth:

Who, when he was reviled, reviled not again; when he suffered, he threatened not; but committed himself to him that judgeth righteously:

Who his own self bare our sins in his own body on the tree, that we, being dead to sins, should live unto righteousness: by whose stripes ye were healed" (1 Peter 2:21-24).

Jesus Christ is our example. He left for all men an example of what God expects from each and everyone of us.

His Baptism

The forerunner of Jesus Christ is John the Baptist. John was chosen and called to prepare the way for the coming ruler of God's people. He was the son of Zacharias and Elizabeth, and a cousin of Jesus (Luke 1:36).

John called the nation unto repentance saying to them: "Repent for the Kingdom of God (heaven) is at hand." John is "The voice of one crying in the wilderness, prepare ye the way of the Lord, make his paths straight ... And all flesh shall see the salvation of the Lord" (Luke 3:4-6). He challenged his hearers to show forth fruits of their repentance by coming to him to be baptized by emersion.

John the Baptist was called and commissioned to baptize for the purpose of introducing the Savior-Messiah to the world:

"And I knew him not: but that he should be made manifest to Israel, therefore am I come baptizing with water" (John 1:31; cf. Luke 2:10; 29-32).

"There was a man sent from God, whose name was John. The same came for a witness, to bear witness of the Light, that all men through him might believe.

He was not that Light, but was sent to bear witness of that Light. That was the true Light, which lighteth every man that cometh into the world" (John 1:6-9; cf. verse 23).

Unlike the New Testament Christian baptism, John's baptism was similar to that of the Old Testament washings

Chapter 6: The Seed of the Woman

which were external, and insufficient to purify the heart. Despite, Jesus Christ also came to be baptized.

Many people came to John to be baptized and Jesus Christ also came to be baptized. John felt unworthy and was reluctant demanding that he rather needed to be baptized by Jesus. In truth, Jesus Christ, unlike us, had no sin to repent and, therefore, needed no baptism, yet as the representative of the people whom He had come to save, He submitted Himself to be baptized:

> "Then cometh Jesus from Galilee to Jordan unto John, to be baptized of him. But John forbad him, saying, I have need to be baptized of thee, and comest thou to me?" (Mathew 3:13-14).

Jesus said to John: "Allow it to be so now: for thus it becometh us to fulfill all righteousness. Then he suffered him" (Mathew 3:15; Mark 1:15; Luke 4:21). Jesus came to fulfill the Old Testament prophesies; or, to be precise, Jesus Christ is the fulfillment.

By submitting to the act of water baptism, Jesus demonstrated His oneness with John's commission of calling the nation unto repentance.

As Jesus was being baptized and praying, the heavens opened, and the Holy Ghost (Spirit) descended in a bodily shape like a dove upon Him and God the Father spoke from heaven:

> "And Jesus, when he was baptized, went up straightway out of the water: and, lo, the heavens were opened unto him, and he saw the Spirit of God descending like a dove, and lighting upon him:
>
> And lo a voice from heaven, saying, This is my beloved Son, in whom I am well pleased" (Mathew 3:16-17; cf. Luke 1:21-22).

John was given the sign that; the man upon whom he shall see the Holy Spirit descending and remaining upon Him, He is the true Messiah. Truly, God does not leave loose ends. Read for yourself what John had to say about Jesus the Christ:

> "And this is the record of John, when the Jews sent priests and Levites from Jerusalem to ask him, Who art thou? And he confessed, and denied not; but confessed, I am not the Christ.
>
> And they asked him, What then? Art thou Elias? And he saith, I am not. Art thou that prophet? And he answered, No.
>
> Then said they unto him, Who art thou? that we may give an answer to them that sent us. What sayest thou of thyself?
>
> He said, I am the voice of one crying in the wilderness, Make straight the way of the Lord, as said the prophet Esaias. And they which were sent were of the Pharisees.
>
> And they asked him, and said unto him, Why baptizest thou then, if thou be not that Christ, nor Elias, neither that prophet? John answered them, saying, I baptize with water: but there standeth one among you, whom ye know not;
>
> He it is, who coming after me is preferred before me, whose shoe's latchet I am not worthy to unloose. These things were done in Bethabara beyond Jordan, where John was baptizing.
>
> The next day John seeth Jesus coming unto him, and saith, Behold the Lamb of God, which taketh away the sin of the world.
>
> This is he of whom I said, After me cometh a man which is preferred before me: for he was before me.
>
> And I knew him not: but that he should be made manifest to Israel, therefore am I come baptizing with water.

Chapter 6: The Seed of the Woman

> And John bare record, saying, I saw the Spirit descending from heaven like a dove, and it abode upon him.
>
> And I knew him not: but he that sent me to baptize with water, the same said unto me, Upon whom thou shalt see the Spirit descending, and remaining on him, the same is he which baptizeth with the Holy Ghost
>
> And I saw, and bare record that this is the Son of God" (John 1:32-33).

The day after Jesus baptism, John was with two of his disciples when Jesus walked by and John said to them: "Behold the Lamb of God" (John 1:36). Immediately, the two disciples left him to follow Jesus.

As God, Jesus Christ did not need this endorsement from the Father, but as a man it was necessary that He be officially introduced, and God chose the time of His baptism to publicly announce His candidacy for the redemption of mankind:

> "And lo a voice from heaven, saying, This is my beloved Son, in whom I am well pleased" (cf. John 12:28-30).

The Father's attesting voice from heaven authenticated the righteous and sinless incarnate Son. God did set a seal to Jesus silent thirty years preceding His baptism. This public witness of the Father indicated that He was fully satisfied with the Son and He would continue to do so. Jesus Christ was about the age of thirty.

The audible voice from heaven being that of the Father and the dove the Holy Spirit, objectively exhibited the "Trinity of the Godhead" (cf. Mathew 17:5). At His baptism: The Father spoke, the Spirit descended, and the Son stood in the water baptized.

Further, this proves that the persons of the trinity are distinct in the Godhead. As the representative new man and "last Adam," Jesus Christ commissioned His church in the name of trinity saying:

"Go ye therefore, and teach all nations, baptizing them in the name of the Father, and of the Son, and of the Holy Ghost:

Teaching them to observe all things whatsoever I have commanded you: and, lo, I am with you always, even unto the end of the world. Amen" (Mathew 28:19-20).

John baptizes with water, but Jesus the Christ as Lord from heaven baptizes with the Holy Spirit and with fire (cf. Mathew 3:11).

His Temptation

The Bible presents Jesus Christ temptation in the wilderness as a fact, and not as a victory over His own thoughts as some unwittingly allege. This was a literal experience for the man who is publicly introduced as the Messiah.

That the new representative man and last Adam be tested and tried is no wonder. The Holy Spirit Himself, who descended upon Jesus at His baptism, led Him into the wilderness where the devil (Satan) ambushed Him when He was weak with fasting.

Jesus was tempted as one of us. He was tempted as a man and not God. As God He could not be tempted (James 1:13). Honestly, the whole temptation would be deemed fraudulent and unnecessary if Satan who is only a creature is to tempt or stand in battle with His Creator and not to talk of winning. Our Lord was there as a man.

The temptations were threefold and they were all directed against His human nature – body, soul, and spirit. As much as testing's of the righteous may come from God, every temptation originate from the devil, and is always directed against the human nature:

"Let no man say when he is tempted, I am tempted of God: for God cannot be tempted with evil, neither tempteth he any man: But every man is tempted, when he is drawn away of his own lust, and enticed.

Then when lust hath conceived, it bringeth forth sin: and sin, when it is finished, bringeth forth death. Do not err, my beloved brethren.

The first temptation was directed at the body and the Lord gave to Satan a befitting answer by quoting the word of God:

"Then was Jesus led up of the Spirit into the wilderness to be tempted of the devil. And when he had fasted forty days and forty nights, he was afterward an hungred.

And when the tempter came to him, he said, If thou be the Son of God, command that these stones be made bread.

But he answered and said, It is written, Man shall not live by bread alone, but by every word that proceedeth out of the mouth of God" (Mathew 4:1-4; cf. Deuteronomy 8:3; John 4:32).

Obedience to the giver of bread is more important than the bread itself. Jesus Christ unlike His counter-part, first Adam and his wife Eve, would not satisfy His natural need by disobeying God (cf. Genesis 3).

The second temptation took place in Jerusalem on the pinnacle of the temple. This was directed toward the soul and again the Lord gave Satan a very good response by quoting the word of God:

"Then the devil taketh him up into the holy city, and setteth him on a pinnacle of the temple,

And saith unto him, If thou be the Son of God, cast thyself down: for it is written, He shall give his angels charge concerning thee: and in their hands they shall bear thee up, lest at any time thou dash thy foot against a stone.

Jesus said unto him, It is written again, Thou shalt not tempt the Lord thy God" (Mathew 4:5-8; cf. Psalm 91:11-12).

In the third temptation, Satan's real motive in the whole temptation event was shown. He took Jesus to a very high mountain and showed Him all the kingdoms of the world. Satan promised to give all to Him if only He would fall down and worship him. This temptation was aimed at His human spirit (cf. John 4: 23-24):

"Again, the devil taketh him up into an exceeding high mountain, and sheweth him all the kingdoms of the world, and the glory of them;

And saith unto him, All these things will I give thee, if thou wilt fall down and worship me.

Then saith Jesus unto him, Get thee hence, Satan: for it is written, Thou shalt worship the Lord thy God, and him only shalt thou serve" (Mathew 4:8-10).

As his custom, Satan always quotes out of context. All who worship Satan are not wise for there is no truth in him. The purpose of Satan is to steal, kill, and destroy the human soul (cf. John 10:10).

All who follow Satan eventually become like him:

"Ye are of your father the devil, and the lusts of your father ye will do. He was a murderer from the beginning, and abode not in the truth, because there is no truth in him. When he speaketh a lie, he speaketh of his own: for he is a liar, and the father of it" (John 8:44).

Satan desires to be worshipped as God. Unfortunately, Satan is not alone in this quest. There are many heads of nations, institutions and religions of the world that desires and commands similar attention. We still have a few statues of those whom we have idolized standing in our town squares.

To worship Satan is to reject the one and only true God. Further, to worship or bow down to a graven image or idol is a rejection of the divine. Further still, the use of religious figures and symbols, incantations, shapes, numbers, and relics can all

Chapter 6: The Seed of the Woman

be forms of Satan worship. Obedience to the word of God is the key to victory over the devils temptation.

Three times, Jesus wielded the sharp sword of God's word against Satan saying: "It is written." Three times, we see truth overpower lies and deception. The secret of success is total submission to God's will:

> "This book of the law shall not depart out of thy mouth; but thou shalt meditate therein day and night, that thou mayest observe to do according to all that is written therein: for then thou shalt make thy way prosperous, and then thou shalt have good success" (Joshua 1:8).

Jesus overcame the power of evil by submitting to the strength and power of God's word through the Holy Spirit.

"Submit yourselves therefore to God. Resist the devil, and he will flee from you," is true for all who would believe by following Christ's example (cf. James 4:7).

Jesus was tempted in every way, yet without sin. He was tempted as a man and He overcame as a man:

> "For we have not an high priest which cannot be touched with the feeling of our infirmities; but was in all points tempted like as we are, yet without sin" (Hebrews 4:15).

Now, because He Himself suffered through His trials and temptations we are guaranteed of His help if we seek His help when tempted:

> "For in that he himself hath suffered being tempted, he is able to succour them that are tempted." (Hebrews 2:18).

Jesus passed the test and Satan's temptations with distinction. So complete was His victory that Satan left him. Jesus Christ returned from this test full of the power of the Holy Spirit and His fame went out through the entire region round about.

Heresy is a denial of the truth; therefore, I call upon you

and every man to examine his or her conscience. I do not think there is an excuse for the failure of both Jews and Gentiles to see Jesus Christ as the promised Savior and Messiah. Take a moment to ponder over this quotation:

> "Every spirit that confesseth that Jesus Christ is come in the flesh or God is become a man is of God: And every spirit that confesseth not that Jesus Christ is come in the flesh is not of God: and this is that spirit of antichrist, whereof ye have heard that it should come; and even now already is it in the world."

The birth of Jesus Christ was predicted almost four thousand years before he was born, yet every prediction came to pass exactly as it was foretold.

Now, considering all the facts so far presented, should not these facts and events of the news of such stupendous birth arrest the attention of the then world? What about ours?

The prophet Job, like Mary, confessed his faith in God by saying: "I know that thou canst do everything" (Job 42:2). What about you and me? Do we believe in the virgin birth?

Admittedly, when was the last time we read or heard of someone whose birth commanded such an enormous activity from both heaven and earth, or even matched that of Jesus Christ? Jesus Christ is the only baby the world has ever known, who did not have a human father. He was born of a woman.

Chapter 7

THE SEED OF ABRAHAM

God promised Abraham saying, "In thee shall all families of the earth be blessed" (Genesis 12:3). Jesus Christ, the promised seed shall come through the line of Abraham. This promise was formalized in a covenant and repeated to Isaac and Jacob. Through the seed of Abraham all the earth shall be blessed:

> "Seeing that Abraham shall surely become a great and mighty nation, and all the nations of the earth shall be blessed in him?" (Genesis 18:18).

The seed of the woman, as promised to Adam and Eve, shall be born of the seed of Abraham. This is the reason Abraham and his descendants were chosen as special people of God. They were chosen as the instrument through which God's appointed Savior would come. They were chosen as apostolic people of God.

The seed of Abraham shall be the star out of Jacob and the scepter out of Israel:

> "shall see him, but not now: I shall behold him, but not nigh: there shall come a Star out of Jacob, and a Sceptre shall rise out of Israel, and shall smite the corners of Moab, and destroy all the children of Sheth" (Numbers 24:17).

Abraham was chosen for a divine purpose, the end of which was the blessing of all people through Jesus Christ who shall come out of his lineage:

> **"And God said, Sarah thy wife shall bear thee a son indeed; and thou shalt call his name Isaac: and I will establish my covenant with him for an everlasting covenant, and with his seed after him" (Genesis 17:19).**

The all-inclusive promise to Abraham was for the whole world of Jews and Gentiles. Through Jesus Christ who is the fountain of life, living water would flow to all who are spiritually thirsty and hunger for righteousness among men of every generation.

God loves all His creatures without exception.

"All His promises and blessings are inclusive without respect of persons" (Romans 2:11; 2 Chronicles 19:7). The promise God made to Abraham looked forward to the one descended Jesus Christ and not the many descendants of Abraham:

> **"Now to Abraham and his seed were the promises made. He saith not, and to seeds, as of many; but as of one, and to thy seed, which is Christ" (Galatians 3:16).**

The central message of the Gospel is the message of "Goodwill towards all men" (Galatians 3:14). Abraham believed God and was obedient to His command.

By faith Abraham obeyed when he was told to leave all, follow the divine command and his obedience through faith was rewarded. Chosen a heathen, he became the father of many nations:

> **"And for this reason, the scripture foreseeing that God would justify the heathen through faith, had the Gospel preached ahead of time to Abraham saying, "in thee shall all nations be blessed" (Galatians 3:8):**

But, beware that despite the all-inclusiveness of promises of the blessing of God, they can only benefit those who believe.

Chapter 7: The Seed of Abraham

All the promises of God in Christ can only be realized by grace through faith in Jesus Christ by the Holy Spirit:

> "That the blessing of Abraham might come on the Gentiles through Jesus Christ; that we might receive the promise of the Spirit through faith" (Galatians 3:14).

The Holy Spirit who is the dispenser of all the graces under the promises of God would only give to those who are justified by faith in the seed.

In fact, the Holy Spirit Himself is also the promise. To inherit the promise, one must exercise faith in the promised Seed of Abraham. We must all, both Jews and Gentiles exercise faith in Jesus Christ to profit (cf. Roman 4:13).

According to Jesus, Abraham saw His days and rejoiced. Abraham saw Jesus Christ and believed in Him:

> "Your father Abraham rejoiced to see my day: and he saw it, and was glad. Then said the Jews unto him, Thou art not yet fifty years old, and hast thou seen Abraham? Jesus said unto them, Verily, verily, I say unto you, Before Abraham was, I am" (John 8:56-58).

Today, we know that almost all the promises God made to Abraham have been fulfilled. And we also know that those still awaiting fulfillment shall also be fulfilled.

Jesus Christ, in His incarnation became a man of Jewish descent from Abraham as promised. He took on Him the seed of Abraham; He was made "like unto his brethren" (Hebrews 2:17):

> "For verily he took not on him the nature of angels; but he took on him the seed of Abraham" (Hebrews 2:16)

In Christ, all things become new (2 Corinthians 5:17). Moses gives way to Christ. The law gives way to grace and the Spirit. The old man gives way to the new man.

In Christ, neither circumcision nor uncircumcision is of any value. What matters to God is a new creature – to be born anew (Galatians 6:15; cf. Romans 2:17-29).

All who join themselves to Jesus Christ become one with Him. They become Abraham's seed, joint heirs and His brethren:

> "And if ye be Christ's, then are ye Abraham's seed, and heirs according to the promise" (Galatians 3:14,29; cf. 1 Corinthians 2:12).

This is not to say God has replaced the Jew with the Christian. No, this is not the case. God still recognizes the natural seeds of Abraham. He has not yet finished with the descendants of Abraham. They still have a major role to play in history. The end is not yet for them.

At the Second Advent of Christ, all Israel shall be saved. At that time Israel shall recognize Jesus Christ for who He is:

> "In his days Judah shall be saved, and Israel shall dwell safely: and this is his name whereby he shall be called, THE LORD OUR RIGHTEOUSNESS" (Jeremiah 23:6).

Jesus Christ is the rightful owner of the land of Israel. It is He who would build God the true Temple. The wars and struggles in the Middle East over the land of promise would only end when He returns to earth.

The nation of Israel no matter how they try would not reclaim the land as given by God to Abraham until they recognize "He who come in the name of Lord" (Genesis 15:18-21). Then all Israel shall be saved:

> "And so all Israel shall be saved: as it is written, There shall come out of Sion the Deliverer, and shall turn away ungodliness from Jacob" (Romans 11:26; cf. Genesis 12:7; 15:18ff).

The purpose of God in Abraham and his natural descendants is Jesus Christ. In Him, the entire world of Jews and Gentiles shall be blessed.

In Jesus Christ, Abraham and his natural descended find

Chapter 7: The Seed of Abraham

their proper places and so is the church. Here is the record of the ancestors of Jesus the Messiah, a descendant of David and of Abraham:

> "The book of the generation of Jesus Christ, the son of David, the son of Abraham. Abraham begat Isaac; and Isaac begat Jacob; and Jacob begat Judas and his brethren;
>
> And Judas begat Phares and Zara of Thamar; and Phares begat Esrom; and Esrom begat Aram; And Aram begat Aminadab; and Aminadab begat Naasson; and Naasson begat Salmon;
>
> And Salmon begat Booz of Rachab; and Booz begat Obed of Ruth; and Obed begat Jesse; And Jesse begat David the king; and David the king begat Solomon of her that had been the wife of Urias . . .
>
> And Jacob begat Joseph the husband of Mary, of whom was born Jesus, who is called Christ" (Mathew 1:1-16).

The very existence of an undisputed genealogy of Jesus Christ dating backward to Jacob, Isaac, and Abraham and even to Adam, and the existence of the nation of Israel proves that the promise made to Abraham and his seeds has been fulfilled.

Jesus Christ is indeed the promised seed of Abraham. Both the descendants of Ishmael and Jacob (Israel) can find consolation and salvation in the seed of Abraham Jesus Christ.

Notes

Chapter 8

THE SEED OF DAVID

Another great prophecy which is fulfilled is that which was made to Israel's King David. The Messiah or the Christ shall descend from the tribe of Judah has been fulfilled.

The Christ or Messiah shall be heir to the throne of King David:

"Concerning his Son Jesus Christ our Lord, which was made of the seed of David according to the flesh. And declared the Son of God with power, according to the Spirit of holiness, by the resurrection from the dead" (Romans 1:3-4).

Jesus Christ was indeed made of the seed of David, but mark that He was not made the Son of God. According to the Scriptures, Jesus Christ was declared the Son of God. The word 'declared' has the meaning of 'appointment' or 'marked out by unmistakable sign' (Acts 10:42; 17:31). The Son of God was not made but eternally is the Son of God.

God promised King David through the prophet Nathan that He would establish the kingdom of his seed forever:

"And when thy days be fulfilled, and thou shalt sleep with thy fathers, I will set up thy seed after thee, which shall proceed out of thy bowels, and I will establish his kingdom. He shall build an house for my name, and I will stablish the throne of his kingdom for ever" (2 Samuel 7:12-13).

Here is the Biblical summary of the genealogy of Jesus Christ, the son of David from the Gospel of Mathew:

> "And Jesse begat David the king; and David the king begat Solomon of her that had been the wife of Urias; And Solomon begat Roboam; and Roboam begat Abia; and Abia begat Asa . . . And Jacob begat Joseph the husband of Mary, of whom was born Jesus, who is called Christ" (Mathew 1:6-16).

Mathew who was writing primarily to the Jewish community connected Jesus with His royal heritage through Joseph, Jesus' legal Father. He shows Jesus Christ as the fulfillment of the covenant promised to both Abraham and David.

Mathew traces the line of Jesus' descent beginning with Abraham through the line of kings who directly followed David:

> "So all the generations from Abraham to David are fourteen generations; and from David until the carrying away into Babylon are fourteen generations; and from the carrying away into Babylon unto Christ are fourteen generations" (Mathew 1:17).

Again, we can add Luke's version of the genealogy of Jesus Christ as an icing on the cake. Luke's genealogy differs from that of Mathew. Luke traces the line of descent through Mary's blood and travels right back passing through David to Adam and working backward from her father Heli, who will be Joseph's father by marriage:

> "And Jesus himself began to be about thirty years of age, being (as was supposed) the son of Joseph, which was the son of Heli . . . which was the son of David, . . . which was the son of Enos, which was the son of Seth, which

Chapter 8: The Seed of David

was the son of Adam, which was the son of God" (Luke 3:23- 38).

Mary, Jesus' actual parent is also a descendant of David. Both Mathew and Luke show that the messianic promises made to David's line were fulfilled in Jesus. Both accounts show that Jesus Christ is indeed the son of Abraham and the Lion of the tribe of Judah. The lion was the emblem of the tribe of Judah, the royal tribe in which the Davidic dynasty ran (Romans 1:3).

The prophet Isaiah centuries after this promise prophesied of the nature of the Davidic Throne under the rule of Messiah saying:

> "Of the increase of his government and peace there shall be no end, upon the throne of David, and upon his kingdom, to order it, and establish it with judgment and with justice from henceforth even for ever. The zeal of the Lord of hosts will perform this (Isaiah 9:7; cf. 11:1-5).

"Now, tracing backward how the Davidic line prophecy was fulfilled, we find the following: both history and the Scriptures testify that historical Jesus Christ was born from the royal line of David as prophesied:

> "And it came to pass in those days, that there went out a decree from Caesar Augustus that all the world should be taxed. (And this taxing was first made when Cyrenius was governor of Syria). And all went to be taxed, every one into his own city.
>
> And Joseph also went up from Galilee, out of the city of Nazareth, into Judaea, unto the city of David, which is called Bethlehem; (because he was of the house and lineage of David).
>
> To be taxed with Mary his espoused wife, being great with child.
>
> And so it was, that, while they were there, the days were accomplished that she should be delivered.

And she brought forth her firstborn son, and wrapped him in swaddling clothes, and laid him in a manger; because there was no room for them in the inn" (Luke 2:1-7).

The book of the generation of Jesus Christ, the son of David, the son of Abraham, and the Son of God testifies to the infallibility of the word of God. Amen.

Peter's great sermon on the day of Pentecost as given in Acts 2:25-36, which is addressed specifically to the men of Israel, has so much to say about Jesus Christ and King David. Let me give you a few examples:

1. This man, Jesus, is "the Lord" – "For David speaketh concerning him, I foresaw the Lord always before my face, for he is on my right hand, that I should not be moved."

2. This man, Jesus, is the "Holy One" – "Therefore did my heart rejoice, and my tongue was glad; moreover also my flesh shall rest in hope: Because thou wilt not leave my soul in hell, neither wilt thou suffer thine Holy One to see corruption."

3. This man, Jesus, is the promised "Christ or Messiah." This man, Jesus, is the promised "King" who would "sit on his throne" – "Men and brethren, let me freely speak unto you of the patriarch David, that he is both dead and buried, and his sepulchre is with us unto this day. Therefore being a prophet, and knowing that God had sworn with an oath to him, that of the fruit of his loins, according to the flesh, he would raise up Christ to sit on his throne; He seeing this before spake of the resurrection of Christ, that his soul was not left in hell, neither his flesh did see corruption.

This man, Jesus, whom King David spoke concerning Him, is both Lord and Christ: "Therefore let all the house of Israel know assuredly, that God hath made the same Jesus, whom ye have crucified, both Lord and Christ" (Acts 2:36).

Chapter 9

THE SON OF MAN

Now, this is where the rubber meets the road. Historical Jesus Christ is God's "Anointed." Jesus the Christ who is the hope of both Jews and Gentiles is no impostor, an enthusiast or liar.

Further, Jesus Christ is not just any man, He is the expected Messiah – the Christ. He had all the characteristics ascribed to the messiah in the prophets and furnished the evidence that He was the Messiah or the Christ sent from God.

According to the prophets, the Messiah shall be the man upon whom the Spirit of the Lord shall rest. The fullness of the Godhead shall dwell in Him bodily (cf. Colossians 2:9 paraphrased):

"And the spirit of the LORD shall rest upon him, the spirit of wisdom and understanding, the spirit of counsel and might, and the spirit of knowledge and of the fear of the LORD" (Isaiah 11:2; cf.).

Unlike the Old and New Testament saints who had the Spirit partially and at certain times, the Spirit shall wholly rest upon the Messiah at all times. He shall literally live in the Spirit and the Spirit in Him.

Although Jesus was fully aware He was the Messiah, He

refrained from using the title and instead chose the title, "Son of man." Son of man was His self-acclaimed name. This was the name or the title He preferred.

In the Gospel, "Son of man," is found on the lips of Jesus about forty times. Yet, despite its frequent usage, it is difficult to know precisely what Jesus meant by this self-designation. The Gospel writers also never explained its significance.

When the audience asked Jesus who is the Son of man? He said to them the Son of man is the light of men. He emphasized on vocation rather than His humanity:

> "Yet a little while is the light with you. Walk while ye have the light, lest darkness come upon you: for he that walketh in darkness knoweth not whither he goeth" (John 12:34-35; cf. Daniel 2:44; 7:13,14,27).

Despite the mystery surrounding this title, some theologians believe that, "Son of man" tends to speak more of His humanity and solidarity with the human race. There are others who claim it binds Jesus to humanity and simultaneously singles Him out from all other men as the sinless One.

Again, the majority, including myself, believe while the name or title may apply to all the aforementioned explanations, it speaks most importantly of the nature of His Messianic mission. For example, when Jesus asked his disciples, saying:

> "Whom do men say that I the Son of man am? Simon Peter answered and said, "Thou art the Christ, the Son of the living God."

> Jesus answered and said unto him, Blessed art thou, Simon Barjona: for flesh and blood hath not revealed it unto thee, but my Father which is in heaven" (cf. Mathew 16:13-17).

Simon Peter's answered and said, "You are the Christ or Messiah," equating "Son of man' with the Messiah and Son of God. Jesus answered and said to him, "Blessed art thou, Simon

Barjona: for flesh and blood hath not revealed it unto thee, but my Father which is in heaven" (cf. Mathew 16:13ff).

Further, Jesus endorsed Peter's accession saying, upon this revelation or truth, "I will build my church:"

> "Then He sternly and strictly charged and warned the disciples to tell no one that He was Jesus the Christ" (Mathew 16:20).

The church would be built upon the foundational truth that "Jesus is the Christ or the Messiah-Lord." Jesus Christ Himself is the "huge rock" on which His church would be built (cf. 1 Corinthians 10:4). No man can be a member or join the church without acknowledging Jesus the Christ as Lord and Savior.

Even the devils acknowledged the truth about His being the Christ and trembled exceedingly:

> "And devils also came out of many, crying out, and saying, Thou art Christ the Son of God. And he rebuking them suffered them not to speak: for they knew that he was the Christ" (Luke 4:41).

The Bible calls the person who denies that Jesus is the Christ a liar. Such a person has all the characteristics and attributes of antichrist.

A false teacher denies that Jesus is the Christ. Further, to admit the truth that Jesus lived, but deny that He is the Christ is to call God a liar. Furthermore, a mere belief in God without a corresponding belief in the Son is false:

> "Who is a liar but he that denieth that Jesus is the Christ? He is antichrist, that denieth the Father and the Son" (1 John 2:22).

Any religion that does not accept Jesus as the Christ does not have a correct view of the Father or know Him. The church or the faithful in Christ are warned to watch out for people who do not preach or teach the doctrine of Christ:

"Whosoever transgresseth, and abideth not in the doctrine of Christ, hath not God. He that abideth in the doctrine of Christ, he hath both the Father and the Son" (2 John 1:9):

"If there come any unto you, and bring not this doctrine, receive him not into your house, neither bid him God speed" (2 John 1:10).

"Beloved, believe not every spirit, but try the spirits whether they are of God: because many false prophets are gone out into the world. Hereby know ye the Spirit of God: Every spirit that confesseth that Jesus Christ is come in the flesh is of God:

And every spirit that confesseth not that Jesus Christ is come in the flesh is not of God: and this is that spirit of antichrist, whereof ye have heard that it should come; and even now already is it in the world" (1 John 4:1-3).

A correct view of the inseparable relationship between God the Father and God the Son is expected of all who believe in the one and only true God the Creator and sustainer of the universe. It is the Father Himself who appointed and anointed His Son as the Savior-Messiah.

John the apostle drove home this point when he testified to the truth saying: "We have seen and do testify that the Father sent the Son to be the Savior of the world" (1 John 4:14). In another place, God testified of the Son saying:

"Thou hast loved righteousness, and hated iniquity; therefore God, even thy God, hath anointed thee with the oil of gladness above thy fellows" (Hebrews 1:9).

Every believer has been anointed with the Holy Spirit, and therefore knows that Jesus is the Christ.

Jesus knew He was the Christ. Using the title Son of man, Jesus made many references indicating He was the Christ who

Chapter 9: The Seed of Man

has come in fulfillment of ancient prophecies. Here a few of His veiled Messianic statements for your personal studies:

1. "The Son of man hath power on earth to forgive sins" (Mathew 9:6).
2. "The Son of man is Lord even of the Sabbath day" (Mathew 12:8).
3. "He that sows the good seed is the Son of man" (Mathew 13:37).
4. "The Son of man shall send forth his angels, and they shall gather out of his kingdom all things that offend, and them which do iniquity" (Mathew 13:41).
5. "For the Son of man shall come in the glory of his Father with his angels; and then he shall reward every man according to his works" (Mathew 16:27).
6. "For the Son of man is come to save that which was lost" (Mathew 18:11).
7. "And he began to teach them, that the Son of man must suffer many things, and be rejected of the elders, and of the chief priests, and scribes, and be killed, and after three days rise again" (mark 8:31).
8. "Whosoever therefore shall be ashamed of me and of my words in this adulterous and sinful generation; of him also shall the Son of man be ashamed, when he cometh in the glory of his Father with the holy angels" (Mark 8:38).
9. "And hath given him authority to execute judgment also, because he is the Son of man" (John 5:27).
10. "Then Jesus said unto them, Verily, verily, I say unto you, Except ye eat the flesh of the Son of man, and drink his blood, ye have no life in you" (John 6:53).
11. "What and if ye shall see the Son of man ascend up where he was before?" (John 6:62).

12. "Then said Jesus unto them, When ye have lifted up the Son of man, then shall ye know that I am he, and that I do nothing of myself; but as my Father hath taught me, I speak these things" (John 8:28).

The Jews were very disappointed in Jesus messianic mission because it was unlike that which they expected. In Jewish thought, the suffering Messiah was never anticipated. A suffering hoped-for-ruler who would deliver Israel from her enemies, especially the Romans and from Rome, and then restore the former glory of the Davidic kingdom was unthinkable.

This misunderstanding contributed largely to His rejection by the religious leaders:

> "And he began to teach them, that the Son of man must suffer many things, and be rejected of the elders, and of the chief priests, and scribes, and be killed, and after three days rise again.
>
> And he spake that saying openly. And Peter took him, and began to rebuke him. But when he had turned about and looked on his disciples, he rebuked Peter, saying, Get thee behind me, Satan: for thou savourest not the things that be of God, but the things that be of men" (Mark 8:31-33).

Jesus Christ made many statements concerning His treatment in the hands of His own people. For example, when He made the statement: "The Son of man goeth as it is written of him" (Mathew 26:24). He was drawing their attention to all that the prophets have foretold in respect to the treatment the Messiah would receive from the hands of His people who were unknowingly fulfilling prophesy by their actions:

> "Then he took unto him the twelve, and said unto them, Behold, we go up to Jerusalem, and all things that are written by the prophets concerning the Son of man shall be accomplished" (Luke 18:31).

Chapter 9: The Seed of Man

According to the Scriptures, Jehovah's servant would be rejected, humbled, afflicted and killed by those to whom He was sent, but He would ultimately emerge victorious and shall be highly be exalted (Mark 16:19; 1 Peter 3:22):

> "And after threescore and two weeks shall Messiah be cut off, but not for himself: and the people of the prince that shall come shall destroy the city and the sanctuary; and the end thereof shall be with a flood, and unto the end of the war desolations are determined" (Daniel 9:26; cf. Psalm 22).

> "I saw in the night visions, and, behold, one like the Son of man came with the clouds of heaven, and came to the Ancient of days, and they brought him near before him" (Daniel 7:13).

For example, Isaiah the prophet made predictions of the suffering Messiah seven hundred years before Christ was born and before His crucifixion. Yet, so precise and detailed was his prophesy that even the critics find it impossible to denounce. Every word of Isaiah's prophecy happened to Jesus Christ.

Here is a progression of what the prophet Isaiah speaking of the suffering Servant-Messiah had to say in Isaiah 53:

1. "For He shall grow before Him" – The eyes of the world would not recognize Him as the Messiah while growing up, but God would. (This is exactly what happened and explains the reason for the myths surrounding the silent years - the years 12 – 30).

2. "A root out of a dry ground" – He would not meet the expectations of the nation. He would be so humble and nothing in His appearance that would attract people to Him.

3. "He is despised and rejected of men" – His birth, life, and death would be subjected to scorn and contempt. Even to date erroneous opinions abound concerning His person.

4. "Surely he hath borne our griefs, and carried our sorrows: yet we did esteem him stricken, smithen of God, and afflicted" – We suppose that He was suffering from some great sins of His own, but He suffered because He carried the sins of the whole world.

5. "He was wounded for our transgressions" – He suffered for our sins. He was slain on account of our sins and no sin of His own.

6. "The Lord hath laid on Him the iniquity of us all" – He was delivered for our offenses (Romans 4:25). It was God Himself who caused the suffering to be vicarious. The Lord gave Him for our sins. He laid on Him the iniquity of us all.

7. "By His strips we are healed" – He was beaten black and blue to secure peace, pardon, forgiveness, and reconciliation for all mankind.

8. "He was oppressed, afflicted, yet opened not His mouth" – He reviled not when reviled. Never complained but submitted His will to Him who is able to raise Him from the dead and He did.

9. "He was taken away from prison and from judgment" – He died as a felon. He was not just killed; He died under a form of law. By oppression and unrighteous proceedings He was taken away. He was cut off from the land of the living and buried with the wicked and even denied Him the privilege of an honorable burial. He was buried in a rich man's tomb.

10. "He had done no violence, neither was any deceit found in his mouth" – He was no murderer, deceiver, thief, political insurrect, no law breaker, but He was treated as one. He was absolutely guiltless.

11. "Yet it pleased the Lord to bruise him; he hath put him to grief: when thou shalt make his soul an offering for

sin" – The whole humiliation of our Lord was one of benevolence and God was very pleased. The Messiah would voluntarily submit Himself to these sorrows which were necessary to show the evil of sin, to illustrate the divine perfections, to show the mercy and justice of God, and because multitudes of lost sinners from all nations shall repent and receive pardon and reconciliation, God was pleased to carry it through.

12. "He shall see the travail of his soul and be satisfied" – He shall live again after He was cut off to see the fruit of His suffering. To see the harvest of souls. He shall look at the glorious result of His work with pleasure.

As prophesied, Jesus Christ career was that of utmost service and suffering with a sure prospect of reward. Yes, "the Son of man hath no where to lay his head," but when it is all said and done, "He shall see of the travail of his soul and shall be satisfied" (cf. (Mathew 8:20; Isaiah 53:10-12).

The Bible declares everyone who denies that Jesus is the Christ a liar. Now, let me ask you this question, do you believe that Jesus is the Christ? The Bible says:

"Whosoever believeth that Jesus is the Christ is born of God: and every one that loveth him that begat loveth him also that is begotten of him"

"For whatsoever is born of God overcometh the world: and this is the victory that overcometh the world, even our faith" (1 John 5:1,4).

Before I conclude this chapter, let me also briefly throw a little light on the role of the Holy Spirit in the personal life and ministry of Jesus the Christ.

Even though Jesus Christ is the Messiah, He is a man. And as man He was only able to fulfill His Messianic mission through the Holy Spirit.

Notes

Chapter 10

JESUS AND THE HOLY SPIRIT

Just as the Scriptures had predicted, Jesus grew to maturity and was filled with wisdom and full of the Spirit:

"And the child grew, and waxed strong in spirit, filled with wisdom: and the grace of God was upon him" (Luke 2:40; cf. verse 52).

Isaiah, the prophet under the unction of the Holy Spirit, spoke of the kind of person the Messiah would be:

"And there shall come forth a rod out of the stem of Jesse, and a Branch shall grow out of his roots:

And the spirit of the LORD shall rest upon him, the spirit of wisdom and understanding, the spirit of counsel and might, the spirit of knowledge and of the fear of the LORD" (Isaiah 11:1-2).

He shall be a descendant from Jesse, shall sit upon the throne of David and He shall totally be inundated by the Spirit throughout His earthly sojourn. This is how the Scriptures foretold His level of dependency:

"And shall make him of quick understanding in the fear of the LORD: and he shall not judge after the sight of his eyes, neither reprove after the hearing of his ears:

> But with righteousness shall he judge the poor, and reprove with equity for the meek of the earth: and he shall smite the earth: with the rod of his mouth, and with the breath of his lips shall he slay the wicked.
>
> And righteousness shall be the girdle of his loins, and faithfulness the girdle of his reins" (Isaiah 11:3-5; cf. Isaiah 42:1-4).

Jesus Christ and the Holy Spirit are distinct but inseparable. Jesus Christ is the Lord. In Exodus 6:12, God calls Himself the Lord: "I am the Lord; that is my name." The Holy Spirit is the Lord: "Now the Lord is that Spirit" (2 Corinthians 3:17).

The union between Jesus and the Spirit is such that the Holy Spirit is also called the Spirit of Christ (1 Peter 1:11). The Spirit was fully responsible for the difference in life and ministry of Jesus Christ.

Jesus quoted the Spirit's presence in His life as a proof of His expiatory mission. "He rejoiced in the Spirit" (Luke 10:21):

> The Spirit of the Lord is upon me, because he hath anointed me to preach the gospel to the poor; he hath sent me to heal the brokenhearted, to preach deliverance to the captives, and recovering of sight to the blind, to set at liberty them that are bruised" (Luke 4:18).
>
> "I can of mine own self do nothing: as I hear, I judge: and my judgment is just; because I seek not mine own will, but the will of the Father which hath sent me" (John 5:30).

The Holy Spirit was responsible for His death. Jesus Christ did not give Himself to be killed because the Scriptures said so. He fully gave Himself first to the Holy Spirit. He would not fulfill His messianic mission by His own will and power:

> "How much more shall the blood of Christ, who through the eternal Spirit offered himself without spot to God, purge your conscience from dead works to serve the living God" (Hebrews 9:14).

Chapter 10: Jesus and the Holy Spirit

Even though He is God, yet in His incarnation He would not do anything without the Holy Spirit. Jesus Christ is at the moment seated at the right hand side of the Throne of Glory, but He dwells in the heart of every born again believer by the Holy Spirit (1 John 4:13).

He continues to carry out His work of saving man by His Spirit. For Peter the apostle to declare Jesus as the Christ was the work of the Holy Spirit. There was no way a sinner like Peter could have known that.

Jesus said when the Spirit comes He would testify of Him, then we who have believed shall also testify (John 15:26):

> "Wherefore I give you to understand, that no man speaking by the Spirit of God calleth Jesus accursed: and that no man can say that Jesus is the Lord, but by the Holy Ghost" (1 Corinthian 12:3; cf. Romans 10:9).

It is only through the Holy Spirit that sinful man can confess and accept Jesus Christ as Lord and Savior. Only the Holy Spirit can testify to the Lordship of Christ within the soul of sinful man. Salvation comes to every man by Jesus Christ through the Holy Spirit by grace.

God gave mankind salvation, Jesus bought it for mankind with His life and the Holy Spirit brings it to everyone who ask for it (1 John 5:11-12):

> "Every spirit that confesseth that Jesus Christ is come in the flesh is of God" (1 John 4:2a).

Worshippers and gospel singers who desire to worship God in truth and in Spirit must be cognizant of the Holy Spirit, for no man can truly worship God apart from the leading of the Holy Spirit:

> "He shall glorify me: for he shall receive of mine, and shall shew it unto you" (John 16:14).

"Anointed," differentiates Jesus Christ from all other religious leaders. As the Anointed One, He was full of the Spirit of God, and He proved His presence by what He did and said. The present work of God on earth is by Jesus Christ through the Holy Spirit:

"For of him, and through him, and to him, are all things" (Romans 11:36).

Without exception, any work of God, if it is to be the work of God, must be of the Holy Spirit. Such work must of a necessity be done by the Holy Spirit through us. Otherwise, such work, no matter how great or grand, would be unprofitable to God. It would be the work of man – a religious hypocrisy.

There is a big difference between doing work for God and God asking you to do something for Him. All that we may desire to do for God and in His name, must be done under the unction of the Spirit. It must be God initiated, God worked, and God glorified.

The Holy Spirit has being instrumental in all the works ever done by man for God or in the name of God. Men like Moses, Gideon, Samson, Elijah and Elisha, Peter, Paul, Philip, Charles Wesley, Charles G. Finney, Kathryn Kuhlman, Maria Woodworth-Etter, and John G. Lake, just to name a few, did what they did and said what they said by the Holy Spirit.

As His disciples, we too can take a serious look at the position and role of the Holy Spirit and emulate. The world would never be won for Christ by preaching alone. We are all witnesses of the results of the shabby work the church has done for Him over the last 2000 years.

Despite all of the media broadcast and missionary work, half of the people in the world today have no knowledge of who Jesus Christ is.

And, until we allow the Spirit to cloth us with himself, get us out of our comfortable castles called church, and preach the Gospel to the unsaved and demonstrate the power of the name of Jesus Christ, the world will never know Jesus Christ, the only Savior for the human race.

Chapter 10: Jesus and the Holy Spirit

That which defines a Christian is the indwelling Holy Spirit (Romans 8:9). If we desire to live right and as God intended, then we must give the Spirit prominence in our life:

> "This I say then, Walk in the Spirit, and ye shall not fulfill the lust of the flesh" (Galatians 5:16).

We can only do the works Jesus did if we allow ourselves to be filled with the Spirit and His power. As a man, Jesus Christ is our living example. He is our only perfect role model.

When Jesus said to His disciples, "Greater things shall ye do," He also said to them, "you shall be clothed with power when the Holy Spirit comes upon you" (Luke 24:49):

> "Upon whom thou shalt see the Spirit descending, and remaining on him, the same is he which baptizeth with the Holy Ghost" (John 1:33b; cf. Acts 1:5).

The church of Jesus Christ would only be His church if the church allows the Spirit to dominate every aspect of her work:

> "For both he that sanctifieth and they who are sanctified are all of one: for which cause he is not ashamed to call them brethren" (Hebrew 2:11).

The Spirit of God, who Himself is the gift of God, comes to every born again believer loaded with supernatural gifts to impart to each of us for the work of God (1 Corinthians 12:7-11). What a difference we can make among our peers and neighbors if we allow the Spirit to fully have His way in our life and service.

Only the Holy Spirit can make known the Son of God to a sinful and dying world. Jesus Christ said when the Spirit comes He would testify of Him:

> "But when the Comforter is come, whom I will send unto you from the Father, even the Spirit of truth, which proceedeth from the Father, he shall testify of me: And ye also shall bear witness, because ye have been with me from the beginning" (John 15:26-27).

God has given the human race both His Son and His Spirit so that we can walk with Him in holiness and righteousness:

"Wherefore I give you to understand, that no man speaking by the Spirit of God calleth Jesus accursed: and that no man can say that Jesus is the Lord, but by the Holy Ghost" (1 Corinthians 12:3).

God is invisible and unsearchable; however, we can know Him by His Holy Spirit whom He has graciously given to all who are born again:

"But as it is written, Eye hath not seen, nor ear heard, neither have entered into the heart of man, the things which God hath prepared for them that love him.

But God hath revealed them unto us by his Spirit: for the Spirit searcheth all things, yea, the deep things of God.

For what man knoweth the things of a man, save the spirit of man which is in him? even so the things of God knoweth no man, but the Spirit of God.

Now we have received, not the spirit of the world, but the spirit which is of God; that we might know the things that are freely given to us of God" (1 Corinthians 2:9-12).

A psychic can be described as a person who tries to solicit information from God outside the Holy Spirit. This is considered an abomination and is forbidden (cf. 1 Samuel 28:1ff).

Further, any man who claims to be a prophet, divine, and or spiritist, must be extremely careful because such intimations may not be from God, but the devils and Satan the prince of demons:

"Beloved, believe not every spirit, but try the spirits whether they are of God: because many false prophets are gone out into the world" (1 John 4:1).

Chapter 10: Jesus and the Holy Spirit

To simply state, neither God nor His Son Jesus Christ can be known outside the Holy Spirit. Further, no man can know the Holy Spirit outside Jesus Christ. Jesus Christ was victorious against sin because He relied 100% on the Spirit. If a man desires to gain complete mastery over sin, he must also prayerfully rely 100% on the Holy Spirit.

In summary, the Son of God became incarnate to be with us and for us. As the second man, last Adam and the representative new man, Jesus Christ is the new role model of the human race. Jesus Christ is every man's example and hero.

Notes

Chapter 11

THE SON OF GOD

If the "Son of man" calls for us to take off our shoes, then, Jesus Christ the "Son of God" calls for us to cast them away for good.

According to the Bible, no man can truly say that Jesus is Lord or the Son of God except by the Spirit of God. Only He who is divine can reveal the Lord to fallen humanity:

"**Whosoever shall confess that Jesus Christ is the Son of God, God dwelleth in him, and he in God**" (1 John 4:15; cf. 5:5).

While both the Gospel according to Mathew and Luke had their eyes on the human lineage and going as far back as to Adam, the Gospel according to John goes further. He goes beyond Adam into eternity past.

John lifts us up far beyond the beginning, before the birth of the first angelic being and into the timeless and endless eternity past as already mentioned:

"In the beginning was the Word, and the Word was with God, and the Word was God. The same was in the beginning with God.

All things were made by him; and without him was not any thing made that was made. In him was life; and the life was the light of men" (John 1:1-4).

As the Word of God Jesus was not just with God, but was God. Further, as the mind of God, He became flesh as the expression of God toward man. But, should anybody think because He is the Word He is just an impersonal quality or faculty in God, the Bible declares Him as the Son:

> "And the Word was made flesh, and dwelt among us, (and we beheld his glory, the glory as of the only begotten of the Father,) full of grace and truth" (John 1:14).

As the eternal Word, He was the eternal Mind, but as the Son, He was at the bosom of the Father, and co-personal with the eternal Father. The Word was not merely from the beginning, but was already in the beginning with God and distinct from God.

Again, should anybody think the Word was inferior to God, the Bible declares the Son and the Father as co-eternal, co-equal and co-Creators.

As the Eternal Word, He is the preserver of both man and the universe:

> "And by him all things consist" (1 Corinthians 1:16-17).

John was absolute in his testimony that Jesus Christ is of a divine origin. He was not just the son of David, Abraham, and Adam, but was indeed the Son of God. Jesus Christ is the Word and the life become flesh.

The testimony of John is a first hand witness to well-proven facts:

> "That which was from the beginning, which we have heard, which we have seen with our eyes, which we have looked upon, and our hands have handled, of the Word of life;

> (For the life was manifested, and we have seen it, and bear witness, and shew unto you that eternal life, which was with the Father, and was manifested unto us;)

Chapter 11: The Son of God

> That which we have seen and heard declare we unto you, that ye also may have fellowship with us: and truly our fellowship is with the Father, and with his Son Jesus Christ. And these things write we unto you, that your joy may be full" (1 John 1:1-4).

In the incarnation, the eternal Word became human or became flesh. The Word became what he was not – the man Jesus Christ.

Historical Jesus the Christ, the man who walked on earth two thousand years ago is the eternal Word become flesh. Never born and never made, He has always existed.

In His relationship to God, Jesus Christ is both the Word and the Son:

> "And . . . his name is called The Word of God" (Revelation 19:13).

No creature has ever seen God at any time in His essence as Spirit. Only the self-existence eternal Son and infinite Spirit has seen God face to face and can reveal Him to mankind. Jesus Christ knows God in a way no man would ever know Him:

> "**No man hath seen God at any time; the only begotten Son, which is in the bosom of the Father, he hath declared him**" (John 1:18; 1 Timothy 6:16).

The expression, "the only begotten" in the above quotation means, "the unique God, or "the unique One." Jesus Christ is the only one with this unique kind of relationship to the eternal Father. 'Begotten,' has never meant that at some point in eternity past God gave birth to Jesus Christ; that is a blasphemy. The "Word became flesh in distinction from beget or create."

Adam, who was also the son of God by creation, was a creature, but Jesus Christ is the eternal Word become Flesh. Jesus is never called a child of God as believers are (cf. 1 John 3:1, 2, 10; 4:9; 5:2). God is not a Father to Jesus in the same sense He is to Christians. Christians are sons of God by adoption.

The invisible Father is brought to view in the visible Son. Jesus said to Philip the disciple: "He that hath seen me hath seen the Father" (John 14:9):

> "All things have been delivered to Me by My Father, and no one knows the Son except the Father. Nor does anyone know the Father except the Son, and the one to whom the Son wills to reveal Him" (Mathew 11:27).

The Fatherhood of God is a relationship that was unthinkable or never known under the Old Covenant. But, Jesus Christ taught all believers to call God Father and even commands all to call and pray to Him as Father.

Philip, a disciple asked Jesus Christ to show them who God the Father is and here was Jesus response:

> "Have I been so long time with you, and yet hast thou not known me, Philip? he that hath seen me hath seen the Father; and how sayest thou then, Show us the Father?

> **Believest thou not that I am in the Father, and the Father in me? the words that I speak unto you I speak not of myself: but the Father that dwelleth in me, he doeth the works"** (John 14:8-10; cf. Mathew 28:20).

God is never lonely. There is constant communication within the Godhead. God is a social being, and so is man whom He has made in His own likeness and image:

> **"But for us there is but one God, the Father, of whom are all things, and we in him; and one Lord Jesus Christ, by whom are all things, and we by him"** (1 Corinthians 8:6; Genesis 1:26a).

When Jesus died on the cross in history, the Bible records that it was God who died for us as an expression of his greater love for the human race:

> **"Hereby perceive we the love of God, because he laid down his life for us: and we ought to lay down our lives for the brethren"** (1 John 3:16).

Chapter 11: The Son of God

Many people outside the Church accuse Christians of serving three God's or gods. However, this is far from the truth. We, the church, do not worship or serve three Gods; God forbid. We worship the one and only true God of the Bible – The One God in three persons (Mathew 28:19). "Our fellowship is with the Father, and with His Son, Jesus Christ" (1 John 3:1b).

In short, to deny the Son is to deny the Father. If anyone denies the Son, he or she does not have the Father:

"Whosoever denieth the Son, the same hath not the Father: he that acknowledgeth the Son hath the Father also" (1 John 2:23).

When God was sending His Son into the world to save humanity, He gave all of His many names under the Old Testament to Him:

"For unto us a child is born, unto us a Son is given: and the government shall be upon His shoulder: and his name shall be called Wonderful, Counselor, The mighty God, The everlasting Father, The Prince of Peace" (Isaiah 9:6; Titus 2:4).

"Therefore let all the house of Israel know assuredly, that God hath made the same Jesus, whom ye have crucified, both Lord and Christ" (Acts 2:36).

The credentials of the eternal Father are the credentials of the eternal Son. The single name "Savior" or "Jesus" given to Him by the Father is a summary of all the names of God. Yahweh is a Savior – He Judges but also saves:

"But my faithfulness and my mercy shall be with him: and in my name shall his horn be exalted" (Psalm 89:24; cf. 72:17).

When you pray to Jesus or call His full name Jesus Christ you have literally evoked all the names of God and all that He stands for. This is the reason why "every knee shall bow and every tongue shall confess Jesus Christ is Lord to the glory of the Father."

When Peter answered; "Thou art the Christ, the Son of the living God." Literally, Peter was saying "You are the expected Messiah and the Lord." Lord is the English name for the Hebrew name Yahweh.

Moses asked what name to use in Egypt and God said, "I AM" (Exodus 3:14-15) which is the same as Yahweh (Jehovah) or Lord (Exodus 6:2-3).

Glory is another title that exclusively belongs to God. God says in Isaiah: "I will not give my glory unto another" (Isaiah 48:11ff); however, under the New Covenant this exclusive name belongs also to the Son. God is one; before and after Him there is no other, which concludes that the Father and Son are one.

Again, when God spoke to Israel through the prophet Isaiah, He said the Son of the virgin shall be called "Emmanuel," which is interpreted "God with us."

It is unthinkable for God to call any mortal man or even the holy angels God, but this is how God sees and acknowledges Jesus Christ.

Again, you would find the meaning of God's proper name "I am," in the name "Emmanuel." God is the only Savior and so are Jesus Christ and the Holy Spirit:

> **"Ye are my witnesses, saith the LORD, and my servant whom I have chosen: that ye may know and believe me, and understand that I am he: before me there was no God formed, neither shall there be after me.**
>
> **I, even I, am the LORD; and beside me there is no saviour. I have declared, and have saved, and I have shewed, when there was no strange god among you: therefore ye are my witnesses, saith the LORD, that I am God"** (Isaiah 43:10-12).

Only God can forgive sins and save sinners and this is exactly what Jesus Christ came to do on earth:

Chapter 11: The Son of God

> "This is a faithful saying, and worthy of all acceptation, that Christ Jesus came into the world to do; to save sinners" (1 Timothy 1:15a).

This exclusive right was witnessed throughout the work of the Son. When Jesus Christ in His incarnation rose again from the dead after His victorious battle against sin and the forces of darkness, God exalted Him to His right hand side and gave Him "a name" What name, "The Lord:"

> "Wherefore God also hath highly exalted him, and given him a name which is above every name. That at the name of Jesus every knee should bow, of things in heaven, and things in earth, and things under the earth;
>
> And that every tongue should confess that Jesus Christ is Lord, to the glory of God the Father" (Philippians 2:9-11).

Beware, Jesus Christ as a man was not crowned with glory until His victory at the cross. It was when He had by Himself cleansed our sins that He was given a place on the right hand of Majesty on high:

> "Who being the brightness of his glory, and the express image of his person, and upholding all things by the word of his power, when he had by himself purged our sins, sat down on the right hand of the Majesty on high" (Hebrews 1:3).

The prophet Daniel foresaw the resurrection and exaltation of the incarnate Son long before it happened and he described what he saw in the following:

> "I saw in the night visions, and, behold, one like the Son of man came with the clouds of heaven, and came to the Ancient of days, and they brought him near before him" (Daniel 7:13).

The position Jesus presently occupies exceeds that of any

angel. Jesus Christ has inherited a more excellent name than they. No angel is qualified to sit on the throne given to the Son. I believe it was this throne that Satan envied in the dateless past that brought about his downfall (cf. Isaiah 14:13-15):

> "Being made so much better than the angels, as he hath by inheritance obtained a more excellent name than they.
>
> For unto which of the angels said he at any time, Thou art my Son, this day have I begotten thee? And again, I will be to him a Father, and he shall be to me a Son?" (Hebrews 1:4-5).

All angels are under command to worship the Son and they do with great joy. Angels are ministering spirits who minister to God and to the heirs of salvation, but to the Son, this is what God had to say:

> "And of the angels he saith, Who maketh his angels spirits, and his ministers a flame of fire. But unto the Son he saith, Thy throne, O God, is for ever and ever: a sceptre of righteousness is the sceptre of thy kingdom.
>
> Thou hast loved righteousness, and hated iniquity; therefore God, even thy God, hath anointed thee with the oil of gladness above thy fellows.
>
> And, Thou, Lord, in the beginning hast laid the foundation of the earth; and the heavens are the works of thine hands: They shall perish; but thou remainest; and they all shall wax old as doth a garment;
>
> And as a vesture shalt thou fold them up, and they shall be changed: but thou art the same, and thy years shall not fail" (Hebrews 1:7-12ff).

God has at the moment delegated all judgment, authority and power to His Son Jesus the Christ. He has given Him authority over heaven, the earth and under the earth.

Chapter 11: The Son of God

Compare the sovereignty of Jehovah under the Old Testament with that of Jesus Christ under the New Testament in the following two quotations:

> "I have sworn by myself, the word is gone out of my mouth in righteousness, and shall not return, That unto me every knee shall bow, every tongue shall swear" (Isaiah 45:23).

> "And Jesus came and spake unto them, saying, All power is given unto me in heaven and in earth" (Mathew 28:18-20).

Unfortunately, the world is full of prophets, messiahs and saviors. Man has invented his own god (s). We have chosen our own prophets; these are men, who claim to have directly heard from God, and we have put them at par with Jesus Christ, but nothing is further from the truth. Jesus Christ is the only Savior the world has and would ever have.

According to the Bible, Jesus Christ is God's final message to the human race. The world must not expect any last prophet, Messiah, Christ, or Savior after Him. The world may or can boast of great prophets and teachers, probably a last prophet, but we all know that none of them can save any man from sin and death. Besides, they all die.

Some are already dead and they probably died as sinners without being saved, and others would soon follow them to the grave, but Jesus Christ who rose from the dead lives on forever. And because He lives, He is able to save to the uttermost all those who come to God for help. His priesthood, unlike that of Aaron is unchangeable. This is what the book to the Hebrews had to say about His unchangeable priesthood:

> "But this man, because he continueth ever, hath an unchangeable priesthood. Wherefore he is able also to save them to the uttermost that come unto God by him, seeing he ever liveth to make intercession for them.
>
> For such an high priest became us, who is holy, harmless,

undefiled, separate from sinners, and made higher than the heavens" (Hebrews 7:24-26).

Only Jesus the Savior can save lost sinners, including all the great prophets known to man. He lives to make intercessions for all who put their faith in Him. Only the sinless man, Christ, can make sinners clean from sin, and He does so with His own blood.

Jesus Christ is the First and the Last. He is the first and the last of His kind (cf. Revelation 22:13):

> "God, who at sundry times and in divers manners spake in time past unto the fathers by the prophets, hath in these last days spoken unto us by his Son, whom he hath appointed heir of all things, by whom also he made the worlds" (Hebrews 1:1-2).

No prophet after Jesus Christ can claim to be prophets from God unless he or she is called by Jesus Christ and gifted by the Holy Spirit with the gift of prophesy. Such a person must be called into the office of the prophet by Jesus Christ and cannot preach anything, but Christ, and Him crucified:

> "But we preach Christ crucified, unto the Jews a stumbling block, and unto the Greeks foolishness" (1 Corinthians 1: 23; cf. Ephesians 4:11; 1 Corinthians 12:10).

To confess that Jesus Christ is the Son of God is to admit that Jesus Christ is Lord or Jesus Christ is God. This is how the Jewish religious community understood the title to mean. Read the following from the book of John:

> "Then the Jews took up stones again to stone him. Jesus answered them, Many good works have I shewed you from my Father; for which of those works do ye stone me?
>
> The Jews answered him, saying, For a good work we stone thee not; but for blasphemy; and because that thou, being a man, makest thyself God.

Chapter 11: The Son of God

> Jesus answered them, Is it not written in your law, I said, Ye are gods? If he called them gods, unto whom the word of God came, and the scripture cannot be broken. Say ye of him, whom the Father hath sanctified, and sent into the world, Thou blasphemest; because I said, I am the Son of God?" (John 10:31-36)

The Jewish leaders understood the implications of this usage and this is the reason why they were extremely unhappy with Jesus. Here is another incident:

> "But Jesus answered them, My Father worketh hitherto, and I work. Therefore the Jews sought the more to kill him, because he not only had broken the Sabbath, but said also that God was his father, making himself equal with God" (John 5:18).

And it was also for this very reason he was crucified. He was killed solely for the purpose that He claimed to be the Son of God or God:

> "And as soon as it was day, the elders of the people and the chief priests and the scribes came together, and led him into their council, saying,
>
> Art thou the Christ? Tell us. And he said unto them, If I tell you, ye will not believe: And if I also ask you, ye will not answer me, nor let me go. Hereafter shall the Son of man sit on the right hand of the power of God.
>
> Then said they all, Art thou then the Son of God? And he said unto them, Ye say that I am. And they said, What need we any further witness? for we ourselves have heard of his own mouth" (Luke 22:66-71; cf. Mathew 7:43).

Further, this is also how the forces of darkness knew Him or understood Him to be. Satan and his coadjutors did everything in their power to obscure His true identity and were always met with a stern rebuke because it is the responsibility of the

Holy Spirit to reveal the full credentials of the incarnate Son of God humanity. Satan and his fallen angels and demons are not qualified to introduce God to the world:

> "And devils also came out of many, crying out, and saying, Thou art Christ the Son of God. And he rebuking them suffered them not to speak: for they knew that he was Christ" (Luke 4:42.)

> "And, behold, they cried out, saying, What have we to do with thee, Jesus, thou Son of God? art thou come hither to torment us before the time?" (Mathew 8:29).

To call Jesus Christ "Lord," is to bear witness to the testimony of God concerning His Son. God has highly exalted Him to the highest position to be a prince and a Savior and to give repentance and remission of sins:

> "Neither is there salvation in any other: for there is none other name under heaven given among men, whereby we must be saved (Acts 4:12; cf. 5:31).

Whosoever believes in Him gets life (John 12:16). Life is in Him and light shines from Him (John 1:4). He is the life and the light for every man that enters this world. As the light, Jesus shines in darkness and darkness cannot comprehend it (John 1:5). From Him all creatures derive their existence and true illumination.

All the treasures of wisdom and knowledge are hidden in Him (Colossians 2:3). It is unfortunate that our school text books talk about almost everybody and everything minus Jesus Christ. Education that excludes the Son of God is incomplete. Jesus Christ fulfills all prophesies.

It appears in our highly charged intellectual society Jesus Christ is non-discussable. Yet, He is the embodiment of all wisdom, knowledge and truth (1 Corinthians 1:24,30).

To all who believe in Him, Jesus gives them power not only to become the sons of God but to live as sons of God:

Chapter 11: The Son of God

> "But as many as received him, to them gave he power to become the sons of God, even to them that believe on his name" (John 1:12).

The early apostles saw Him and claimed Him to be the Son of God. The fourth Gospel especially is written to reveal Jesus as the Christ and whosoever believeth is born of God or has eternal life:

> "But these are written, that ye might believe that Jesus is the Christ, the Son of God; and that believing ye might have life through his name" (John 20:31; Acts 9:20; Romans 1:3; 2 Corinthians 1:19; Hebrews 7:2-4).

> "These things have I written unto you that believe on the name of the Son of God; that ye may know that ye have eternal life, and that ye may believe on the name of the Son of God" (1 John 5:13).

Again, this is how disciples two millennium after His departure including me see Him and claimed Him to be – "the Son of the living God."

It is extremely important as Christians that each and every one of us re-examine ourselves to see if we are still in the faith. I believe it is about time all those who call themselves Children of God quit doubting the humanity and the deity of Jesus Christ.

We ought to "look to ourselves, that we lose not those things which we have wrought, but that we receive a full reward:

> "That if you confess with your mouth, "Jesus is Lord," and believe in your heart that God raised him from the dead, you will be saved. For it is with your heart that you believe and are justified, and it is with your mouth that you confess and are saved" (Romans 10:9-10)

> "Whosoever shall confess that Jesus is the Son of God, God dwelleth in him, and he in God" (1 John 4:15).

> "Who is he that overcometh the world, but he that believeth that Jesus is the Son of God?" (1 John 5:5).

> "Whosoever believeth that Jesus Christ is the Christ is born of God: "He that hath the Son hath life; and he that hath not the Son of God hath not life" (1 John 5:12; Colossians 3:4).

God Himself bears witness of the deity of His Son. The eternal record reveals that God has given to humanity life and that this life is in His Son and anyone who denies this truth or claim makes God a liar:

> "If we receive the witness of men, the witness of God is greater: for this is the witness of God which he hath testified of his Son. He that believeth on the Son of God hath the witness in himself: he that believeth not God hath made him a liar; because he believeth not the record that God gave of his Son" (1 John 5:9-10).

Three times, God spoke audibly and publicly from heaven introducing His Son to the world:

> "And Jesus, when he was baptized, went up straightway out of the water: and, lo, the heavens were opened unto him, and he saw the Spirit of God descending like a dove, and lighting upon him: And lo a voice from heaven, saying, This is my beloved Son, in whom I am well pleased" (Mathew 3:16-17).

> "While he yet spake, behold, a bright cloud overshadowed them: and behold a voice out of the cloud, which said, This is my beloved Son, in whom I am well pleased; hear ye him" (Mathew 17:5).

> "Father, glorify thy name. Then came there a voice from heaven, saying, I have both glorified it, and will glorify it again" (John 12:28).

God the Father would not do anything without God the Son and neither would God the Son do anything without the

Chapter 11: The Son of God

God the Father and God the Holy Spirit. The Holy Spirit would not do anything without Jesus Christ (1 John 5:20; 1 Timothy 6:15):

> "For there are three that bear record in heaven, the Father, the Word, and the Holy Ghost: and these three are one" (1 John 5:7).

Let it be known that if we deny that Jesus Christ is the Son of God we stand in danger of losing our soul.

According to the Scriptures, it is extremely important for every man to know that, " the Son of God is come, and hath given us an understanding, that we may know him that is true, and we are in him that is true, even in his Son Jesus Christ.

Jesus Christ is the true God, and eternal life" (1 John 5:20). "No man hath seen God at any time, the only begotten Son, which is in the bosom of the Father, he hath declared him" (John 1:18; cf. 17:26). All the truths of pre-existence, deity and Messiahship are in the Son:

> "And the LORD shall be king over all the earth: in that day shall there be one LORD, and his name one" (Zechariah 14:9).

Jesus Christ is the Divine nature become incarnate. He is God come in the flesh. The Holy Spirit Himself bears witness to this truth. If we receive the witness of men, the witness of God is greater. Jesus Christ came not by water only, but by water and blood:

> "And every spirit that confesseth not that Jesus Christ is come in the flesh is not of God: and this is that spirit of antichrist, whereof ye have heard that it should come; and even now already is it in the world" (1 John 4:3).

The fact of Jesus Christ being the Son of God cannot be over emphasized, for if He is not then let us trash the New Testament and declare God a liar because it was He who declared Him to be so.

In summary, historical Jesus Christ of Nazareth is the eternal Son, Israel's Messiah and Jehovah; the Savior and hope of everyone in the world. He who is the Savior of the world is the Maker of the world.

Jesus Christ the only Son of God is the true God, and eternal life – fully divine and fully man (cf. 1 John 5:20). God the Father and Son are distinct, but inseparable. Jesus the Christ is God.

Chapter 12

HE SPOKE WITH AUTHORITY

I have intentionally separated His claims from the authority with which Jesus Christ communicated because I believe it deserves a separate chapter for how can any student of the New Testament escape that? His words were powerful.

"No man spoke like Jesus Christ." His audiences were spellbound and astonished at His doctrines. Listeners left His presence with deep fear and uncertainty of His person asking themselves; "what manner of man is this" (Mathew 8:27):

> "And it came to pass, when Jesus had ended these sayings, the people were astonished at his doctrine" (Mathew 7:28; cf. 22:33).

The outstanding feature of His teaching was His authority. He delivered His message with divine approval and authority. Such straightforward preaching, based on the depth of His impeccable life and mission, was in contrast to that of the scribes.

The scribes were the copyists of the law and the theologians of the day. They relied on the tradition for their authority, but this was not the case with Jesus the Christ. He was His own authority. Jesus knew where He had come from, what His purpose was on earth, and where He was going after mission accomplishment.

Everyone who heard Him marveled and wondered at the gracious words which came out of His mouth. Multitudes spent days in the harsh and dry plains of Palestine just to hear Him speak (cf. Mathew 15:32):

> **"And all bare him witness, and wondered at the gracious words which proceeded out of his mouth. And they said, Is not this Joseph's son?" (Luke 4:22).**

He taught the people in a manner that was quite different from that of the Jewish teachers. Jesus Christ taught them as one having power and authority (Mark 1:22). His words were with power:

> **"And they were astonished at his doctrine: for his word was with power" (Luke 4:32).**

> **"And they were astonished at his doctrine: for he taught them as one that had authority, and not as the scribes" (Mark1:22).**

Even today many people express awe and shock when they read the sayings of Jesus Christ from the Bible with the exception of the unaided minds. The key to understanding and appreciating His sayings lay with the Holy Spirit (John 16:13ff).

His words are the very embodiment of truth. Jesus called for allegiance unparalleled. Take a look at a few examples from the book of Mathew:

> **"He that loveth father or mother more than me is not worthy of me: and he that loveth son or daughter more than me is not worthy of me" (Mathew 10:37).**

> **"And I will give unto thee the keys of the kingdom of heaven: and whatsoever thou shalt bind on earth shall be bound in heaven: and whatsoever thou shalt loose on earth shall be loosed in heaven" (Mathew 16:19).**

Chapter 12: He Spoke with Authority

> "For whosoever will save his life shall lose it: and whosoever will lose his life for my sake shall find it" (Mathew 16:25).

> "And every one that hath forsaken houses, or brethren, or sisters, or father, or mother, or wife, or children, or lands, for my name's sake, shall receive an hundredfold, and shall inherit everlasting life" (Mathew 19:29).

He spoke with such confidence and exactness of his future in such a way that left His audiences no choice but to accept or turn and bite. They were compelled to either accept Him as the Christ or reject Him as one who is beside Himself:

> "And then shall appear the sign of the Son of man in heaven: and then shall all the tribes of the earth mourn, and they shall see the Son of man coming in the clouds of heaven with power and great glory" (Matthew 24:30)

> "When the Son of man shall come in his glory, and all the holy angels with him, then shall he sit upon the throne of his glory" (Mathew 25:31).

> "But of that day and that hour knoweth no man, no, not the angels which are in heaven, neither the Son, but the Father" (Mark 13:32).

> "For as the lightning, that lighteneth out of the one part under heaven, shineth unto the other part under heaven; so shall also the Son of man be in his day" (Luke 17:24).

His words were transcended and everlasting. They were words which traveled beyond His time. He spoke as one who lived in the past, present and future and as a man who lives forever to make His words and promises good:

> "I am with you always, even to the end of the age" (Mathew 28:20; cf. 24-25).

Jesus Christ was a man in full control of His words. He spoke the truth at all times and with great compassion. He spoke of His death and resurrection with great detail well in advance. He talked of His impending death as a blessing and essential for the salvation of all humanity:

> "For as Jonas was three days and three nights in the whale's belly; so shall the Son of man be three days and three nights in the heart of the earth(John 12:40).

> "And as they came down from the mountain, Jesus charged them, saying, Tell the vision to no man, until the Son of man be risen again from the dead" (Mathew 17:9).

> "Behold, we go up to Jerusalem; and the Son of man shall be betrayed unto the chief priests and unto the scribes, and they shall condemn him to death" (Mathew 20:18).

> "The Son of man goeth as it is written of him: but woe unto that man by whom the Son of man is betrayed! it had been good for that man if he had not been born" (Mathew 26:24).

> "The Son of man must suffer many things, and be rejected of the elders and chief priests and scribes, and be slain, and be raised the third day" (Luke 9:22).

> "Then said Jesus unto them, When ye have lifted up the Son of man, then shall ye know that I am he, and that I do nothing of myself; but as my Father hath taught me, I speak these things" (John 8:28).

Jesus spoke as one who has all the facts and the power to execute His will. Power was His at all times to dispense at will. He saw Himself as the only hope of mankind and called men to acknowledge it to be so.

What He said and did proved who He said He was. Jesus promised He would return to earth, so let us wait for Him because He shall surely come. Here is a piece of what He said concerning His Second Coming:

> **"Immediately after the tribulation of those days shall the sun be darkened, and the moon shall not give her light, and the stars shall fall from heaven, and the powers of the heavens shall be shaken:**
>
> **And then shall appear the sign of the Son of man in heaven: and then shall all the tribes of the earth mourn, and they shall see the Son of man coming in the clouds of heaven with power and great glory.**
>
> **And he shall send his angels with a great sound of a trumpet, and they shall gather together his elect from the four winds, from one end of heaven to the other"** (Mathew 24:29-31; cf. 26:64; Acts 1:11).

The note of authority in the Sermon on the Mount is a warning that no man can ignore or reject Jesus teaching without consequences. Beyond its moral, ethical, and spiritual teaching is the person of the Preacher Himself. He calls attention to Himself as the focal point of His entire message:

> **"Again, ye have heard that it hath been said by them of old time, Thou shalt not forswear thyself, but shalt perform unto the Lord thine oaths: But I say unto you, Swear not at all; neither by heaven; it is God's throne** (Mathew 5:33-34).

In conclusion, no man alive or dead ever spoke with authority like Jesus Christ. He was a man of authority and spoke with authority.

With the exception of the man from heaven who claims to be fully God and fully man, Jesus Christ, I do not think any man can truly say: "Heaven and earth shall pass away, but my words shall not pass away."

Notes

Chapter 13

His Own Claims

The claims of Jesus are such that no man can accept them unless first, one accepts Him for all that He claims to be. Otherwise, Jesus shall be seen as a man with a big mouth, blasphemer or crazy as some unaided minds still think of Him.

Let me start with one of the most profound claims that Jesus made which I believe eclipsed all others. This was His constant usage of the divine name, "I am." Jesus did not only use this name one time but was His habit of personalizing the divine name.

In the Gospel of John alone, Jesus uses "I am" twenty three times. A typical example was His conversation with the woman from Sychar in Samaria:

> **"The woman saith unto him, I know that Messiah cometh, which is called Christ: when he is come, he will tell us all things. Jesus said unto her, I that speak to thee am he"** (John 4:25-26; cf. 6:20,35,41,48,51; 8:12,18,24,28,58; 10:7,9,11,14, 11:25; 13:19; 14:6; 15:1,5; 23:5,6,8).

"I am," translated in Greek is Ego eimi. Both ego and eimi means I am. The former emphasizes "I" and the latter "am." Thus ego eimi expresses personal being in the strongest possible way. "What Jesus said to the Samaritan woman was the use of ego eimi with the maximum implication."

Using the name I am, Jesus was saying to this woman I, who is talking to you, am (the divine) or I am the expected Messiah – I am the Christ, the one in whom Yahweh, the God of Abraham, Isaac and Jacob is fully revealed.

This is the way the Jewish community understood His repeated usage of this revered holy name of God. So, you can understand why they were infuriated and gnashed their teeth at Him.

Technically, Jesus Christ was by this repetitive personal usage claiming to be equal with God or God. He claimed equality with God almost at all levels. He claimed every honor due to God.

Carefully, read the following example and deduce for yourself, if these sayings of His are that of a mere man:

> "Then answered Jesus and said unto them, Verily, verily, I say unto you, The Son can do nothing of himself, but what he seeth the Father do: for what things soever he doeth, these also doeth the Son likewise.
>
> For the Father loveth the Son, and sheweth him all things that himself doeth: and he will shew him greater works than these, that ye may marvel.
>
> For as the Father raiseth up the dead, and quickeneth them; even so the Son quickeneth whom he will.
>
> For the Father judgeth no man, but hath committed all judgment unto the Son: That all men should honour the Son, even as they honour the Father. He that honoureth not the Son honoureth not the Father which hath sent him.
>
> Verily, verily, I say unto you, He that heareth my word, and believeth on him that sent me, hath everlasting life, and shall not come into condemnation; but is passed from death unto life.

Chapter 13: His Own Claims

> Verily, verily, I say unto you, The hour is coming, and now is, when the dead shall hear the voice of the Son of God: and they that hear shall live.
>
> For as the Father hath life in himself; so hath he given to the Son to have life in himself; And hath given him authority to execute judgment also, because he is the Son of man.
>
> Marvel not at this: for the hour is coming, in the which all that are in the graves shall hear his voice,
>
> And shall come forth; they that have done good, unto the resurrection of life; and they that have done evil, unto the resurrection of damnation.
>
> I can of mine own self do nothing: as I hear, I judge: and my judgment is just; because I seek not mine own will, but the will of the Father which hath sent me" (John 5:19-30).

Another example is the incident at the Sea of Galilee. The former fishermen now made disciples of Jesus were out of their wits in their battle against the ferocious storms at sea. As if this was not terrifying enough, Jesus came walking on the sea towards them?

They screamed in fear and right away Jesus spoke to them using the divine name. Jesus said to them, "Be of good cheer it is I, the all powerful God who is with you, do not be afraid."

> "Be of good cheer; it is I; be not afraid" (Mathew 14:27; cf. verses 28-33).

What followed soon after fully supported His claim. Jesus granted Peter the power and authority to walk on the sea. Can you imagine the wonder in the faces of these disciples in the making?

They were convinced beyond all doubt that the man walking on the sea and the man they have come to love is no other man than the Son of God – Israel's Messiah. Read for yourself what they did to Jesus Christ when He came into the boat:

> "Then they that were in the ship came and worshipped him, saying, Of a truth thou art the Son of God" (Mathew 14:33; cf. Revelation 22:9).

They followed their faith by giving Him the worship and honor that is only due to God and Jesus accepted it. He accepted the worship that even holy angels revere (cf. Revelation 19:10).

This event at sea brings to mind the debate Jesus had with the Jewish leaders in John 8. Jesus claimed Abraham rejoiced to see His day and saw it and the Jews, especially, the leaders were overly offended.

They responded by saying, "thou art not yet fifty years old, and thou hast seen Abraham?" Jesus response immediately sparked an attempt to stone Him and this is what Jesus said to them:

> "Verily, verily, I say unto you, before Abraham was, I am" (John 8:58).

But, this was no boast on the part of Jesus Christ. God Himself testifying of His Son (servant) in the Old Testament had this to say:

> "Ye are my witnesses, saith the LORD, and my servant whom I have chosen: that ye may know and believe me, and understand that I am he: before me there was no God formed, neither shall there be after me. I, even I, am the LORD; and beside me there is no saviour.
>
> I have declared, and have saved, and I have shewed, when there was no strange god among you: therefore ye are my witnesses, saith the LORD, that I am God. Yea, before the day was I am he; and there is none that can deliver out of my hand: I will work, and who shall let it?" (Isaiah 43:10-13).

Clearly, from this prophecy we can again deduce that the Yahweh and Savior of the Old Testament is Jesus the Christ of

Chapter 13: His Own Claims

the New Testament. God sent Him into the world of mankind so that we may know that He is the only One and true God and be reconciled to Him through His only mediator (cf. 1 Timothy 2:5).

Here are few of His "I am" claims for your personal study:

1. "I am the living bread which came down from heaven: if any man eat of this bread, he shall live for ever" (John 6:51; cf. verse 41).
2. "I am the light of the world" (John 8:12).
3. "I am the door of the sheep" (John 10:7-9).
4. "I am the good shepherd, and know my sheep, and am known of mine" (John 10:11-14).
5. "I am the resurrection, and the life: he that believeth in me, though he were dead, yet shall he live" (John 11:25).
6. "I am the way, the truth, and the life: no man cometh unto the Father but by me" (John 14:6).
7. "I am the vine, ye are the branches: He that abideth in me, and I in him, the same bringeth forth much fruit: for without me you can do nothing (John 15:5).

Jesus was teaching during one of the Feast of Tabernacles, and the common people were debating among themselves if He was indeed the Christ. But, they were overheard by the Jewish leaders. Afraid of their own positions, these leaders immediately sent officers or soldiers to arrest Jesus. However, the soldiers after hearing Jesus speak, had a change of mind and decided not to arrest Him.

Returning to those who sent them without Jesus, they were questioned why they failed to bring Him and here was their reply:

"Never man spake like this man" (John 7:45-46).

Probably, if I were one of these officers, my answer might be the same, so I dare not blame them. I am fifty three years old, but I cannot think of any man in history that has ever come close to the claims of Jesus Christ and not to talk of His works and flawless life.

Recognizing that the Jews, especially the leaders would not accept His testimony, Jesus called upon God as His witness. Only He who claims to be God can call upon God as a witness.

Jesus Christ also called three other witnesses: His own works, John the Baptist, and the Scriptures. Examine the following:

> "But I have greater witness than that of John: for the works which the Father hath given me to finish, the same works that I do, bear witness of me, that the Father hath sent me" (John 5:36).

> "And the Father himself, which hath sent me, hath borne witness of me. Ye have neither heard his voice at any time, nor seen his shape. And ye have not his word abiding in you: for whom he hath sent, him ye believe not" (John 5:37-38; cf. 5:34-35).

> "Search the scriptures; for in them ye think ye have eternal life: and they are they which testify of me. And ye will not come to me, that ye might have life. I receive not honour from men. But I know you, that ye have not the love of God in you. I am come in my Father's name, and ye receive me not: if another shall come in his own name, him ye will receive" (John 5:39ff).

The bad news is that the Jewish leaders understood His claims alright, yet, they rejected Him. Who knows why? Probably, they could not contain Him in their religious pride and arrogance. His sinless and shining life revealed the dark corners of their own hypocritical life. Jesus was simply too much for their religious pride.

Whether the claims of Jesus Christ are the sayings of men or that of God is up to each of us also to decide. Believe it or not, the

Chapter 13: His Own Claims

claims of Jesus are claims of a mere man who is endowed with the gifts of the Spirit or that of a prophet speaking the words of God. They can only be the claims of a man who is God.

Peter said the words of Jesus Christ are "words of eternal life" (John 6:68). He witnessed Jesus forgive sin and demonstrated His authority to do by healing the sick, raising the dead and casting out devils.

Read the following example:

> "And, behold, they brought to him a man sick of the palsy, lying on a bed: and Jesus seeing their faith said unto the sick of the palsy; Son, be of good cheer; thy sins be forgiven thee.
>
> And, behold, certain of the scribes said within themselves, this man blasphemeth. And Jesus knowing their thoughts said, Wherefore think ye evil in your hearts? For whether is easier, to say, Thy sins be forgiven thee; or to say, Arise, and walk?
>
> But that ye may know that the Son of man hath power on earth to forgive sins, (then saith he to the sick of the palsy,) Arise, take up thy bed, and go unto thine house. And he arose, and departed to his house" (Mathew 9:2-6).

Jesus was fully aware of His sinlessness (Mathew 11:27; 12:8,32,40). At one point He said to the people: "Which of you convinceth me of sin? And if I say the truth, why do ye not believe me? He that is of God heareth God's words: ye therefore hear them not, because ye are not of God" (John 8:46-47).

He said He would be recognized for who He claims to be when He raises from the dead. Jesus Christ resurrection from the dead is the single most powerful proof of the success and completeness of His Messianic mission. It overshadows all that He did and said:

> "Then said Jesus unto them, When ye have lifted up the Son of man, then shall ye know that I am he, and that I

do nothing of myself; but as my Father hath taught me, I speak these things" (John 8:28cf. Mathew 11:2-6; cf. 16:16,20; Luke 3:15).

Today billions of people are His followers and daily the list grows. The dead are being raised back to life and all kinds of diseases and infirmities healed in His name across the nations. His words have come true.

As already stated, the devils, though evil in their motives are not left out in the parade of testimonies proving His claims. Terrified by His presence they could not keep still. They came out of many, crying out:"

> "Why are you interfering with us, Jesus of Nazareth? Have you come to destroy us? I know who you are—the Holy One sent from God! Jesus cut him short. "Be quiet! Come out of the man," he ordered" (Mark 1:24-25,34; cf. Luke 4:41; Mathew 8:28-29).

Jesus Christ aligned Himself with God as the only one who can give eternal life. He claimed: "He came that mankind might have life, and that they might have it more abundantly" (John 10:10 paraphrased).

He claimed no man can see or know God unless he first has a relationship with Him:

> "And this is life eternal, that they might know thee the only true God, and Jesus Christ, whom thou hast sent" (John 17:3).

> "I am the resurrection, and the life: he that believeth in me, though he were dead, yet shall he live: And whosoever liveth and believeth in me shall never die. Believest thou this?" (John 11:46-47).

He claimed to be the only one man who can decide the fate of every man. The decision as to who enters the kingdom of God solely rest upon Him. The kingdom of God or heaven is His to appoint (Luke 22:29).

Chapter 13: His Own Claims

He claimed to possess the keys of heaven, death and hell. He said at the end of the ages; it would be up to Him to decide the final destiny of all creatures:

> "All things are delivered unto me of my Father: and no man knoweth the Son, but the Father; neither knoweth any man the Father, save the Son, and he to whomsoever the Son will reveal him" (Mathew 11:27).

Jesus claimed He Himself is the fulfillment of all the Old Testament prophesies – he came to fulfill all that was said of Him in prophesy.

The Old Testament ceremonies and laws as shadows are lost in Him as the substance and cease to be binding. They are fulfilled in Him. He did not come to do away with the law but to give its true and intended meaning:

> "Think not that I am come to destroy the law, or the prophets: I am not come to destroy, but to fulfil" (Mathew 5:17; cf. 1:22; 2:15,17, 23; 4:14; 8:17 12:17; 13:35; 21:4; 26:56; 27:9,35).

Space and time would not permit me to quote all the claims of Jesus but here are a few for your personal studies.

1. "Ye are from beneath; I am from above: ye are of the world; I am not of this world" (John 8:23).

2. "When ye have lifted the Son of man, then ye shall know that I am he" (John 8:28).

3. "Verily, verily, I say unto you, if a man keep my saying, he shall never see death" (John 8:51).

4. "The hour is coming, and now is, when the dead shall hear the voice of the Son of God: and they that hear shall live" (John 5:25).

5. "He that heareth my word, and believeth on him that sent me, hath everlasting life, and shall not come into condemnation; but is passed from death unto life" (John 5:25).

6. "If thou knewest the gift of God, and who it is that saith to thee, Give me to drink; thou wouldest hath asked of him, and would have given thee living water" (John 4:10).

7. Hereafter shall the Son of man sit on the right hand of the power of God" (Luke 22:69).

8. "Heaven and earth shall pass away, but my words shall not pass away" (Mathew 24:35).

9. "All power is given unto me in heaven and in earth. Go ye therefore, and teach all nations, baptizing them in the name of the Father, and of the Son, and of the Holy Ghost" (Mathew 28:18-19).

10. "And now, O Father, glorify thou me with thine own self with the glory which I had with thee before the world was" (John 17:5).

11. "No man can come to me, except the Father which hath sent me draw him: and I will raise him up at the last day (John 6:44).

Again, ponder over the following as my summary to this chapter.

1. "But as many as received him, to them gave he power to become the sons of God, even to them that believe on his name" (John 1:12).

2. "No man hath seen God at any time, the only begotten Son, which is in the bosom of the Father, he hath declared him" (John 1:18).

3. "And no man hath ascended up to heaven, but he that came down from heaven, even the Son of man which is in heaven" (John 3:13).

4. "Labour not for the meat which perisheth, but for that meat which endureth unto everlasting life, which the Son of man shall give unto you: for him hath God the Father sealed" (John 6:27).

Chapter 13: His Own Claims

5. "Then Jesus said unto them, Verily, verily, I say unto you, Except ye eat the flesh of the Son of man, and drink his blood, ye have no life in you" (John 6:53).

6. "Verily, verily, I say unto you, The hour is coming, and now is, when the dead shall hear the voice of the Son of God: and they that hear shall live. For as the Father hath life in himself; so hath he given to the Son to have life in himself" (John 5:19,26).

Personally, I do not think that any religious leader, prophet, priest, guru, or Imam has ever made and can make such claims as that of Jesus Christ.

No mere human being by any stretch of the imagination can claim that his relationship to humanity decides the fate or the final destiny of the rest of mankind, and neither can any mere man say he is the object of saving faith.

Notes

Chapter 14

His Teachings

People from all walks of life and educational fortitudes have and still learn wisdom and knowledge from His teachings. Nations, especially the west owes much of their reforms to Jesus Christ. People of every generation, gender and culture have found consolation, knowledge and wisdom from His words and doctrines.

Jesus is "The master" no matter the subject. He talked almost about everything – every issue that faces mankind, from that which is sacred to the secular.

He spoke to people of all ages, class and gender. Take for example, His sermons on the mount which contain ten components from the book of Mathew (chapters 5-7):

1. The Beatitudes
2. Moral Standards
3. Religious Motives
4. Mammon Worship
5. Temporal Cares.
6. Social Discernment
7. Encouragements

8. Summary Statement
9. The two Ways
10. Warnings on Falsehood

Jesus teachings are incomparable in history. He gave a lengthy discourse on the signs of the end times, which I believe every person should take the time to read in Mathew 24, especially world leaders.

The main subject of His teaching and preaching was the "Kingdom of God." The Kingdom of God and the Kingdom of heaven mean one and the same and can be used interchangeably.

Jesus Christ went from city to city teaching and preaching that His presence is a sign that the Kingdom has arrived. He spoke openly daily in the temple, synagogues, open countryside, the sea side and wherever the Jews resorted:

> **"And Jesus went about all Galilee, teaching in their synagogues, and preaching the gospel of the kingdom, and healing all manner of sickness and all manner of disease among the people" (Mathew 4:23; cf. 9:35; John 18:20).**

No man taught like Jesus Christ the people said. He spoke as having heard from the Father; therefore speaks the very words of God. He said His teachings were not of His own, but that of the Father, and quoted the prophecy of the prophet Isaiah to support His claim:

> **"And all thy children shall be taught of the LORD; and great shall be the peace of thy children" (Isaiah 54:13).**

His teachings were attested to by the populace, even His enemies acknowledged the truth and the depth of wisdom in His teachings:

> **"We know that thou art true, and teachest the way of God in truth, neither carest thou for any man: for thou regardest not the person of men" (cf. Matthew 22:16; Mark 12:14).**

Chapter 14: His Teachings

His audience saw Him as a man possessing the truth and the dispenser of truth:

> **"The same came to Jesus by night, and said unto him, Rabbi, we know that thou art a teacher come from God: for no man can do these miracles that thou doest, except God be with him"** (John 3:2).

His teaching method was simple. As already said, He was truthful and no man pleaser. At the beginning of His ministry, he taught the people plainly, but later He began to teach them in parables with the exception of His disciples because the populace together with their leaders rejected His teachings (cf. Mathew 13:11):

> **"Therefore speak I to them in parables: because they seeing see not; and hearing they hear not, neither do they understand"** (Mathew 13:13; cf. verse 11-12).

The parables veiled the truth from the unbeliever, but were plain to the sincere disciple. Truth comes with responsibility.

John the Baptist, the forerunner and a cousin to Jesus Christ was actually the torch bearer of Jesus teaching on the Kingdom. Dressed like one of the ancient prophets in goat and Carmel skin, he renounced the whole Jewish system of political and hypocritical religious dogma and called on the people to "repent for the kingdom of heaven is at hand" (Mathew 3:2).

He demanded the people prove their repentance by being baptized, and called upon the baptized to bring forth fruits worthy of repentance. Many people from all walks of life came to him to be baptized at the river Jordan.

His was a radical movement for no prophet had demanded this of the Jews before. To John, being a pious Jew was not enough. He even rebuked Herod, the ruler of Galilee for taking his brother's wife which later caused him his life.

But, before his death, Jesus Christ stepped out of the shadows to the center stage. His message of the kingdom was a direct sequel to that of John the Baptist:

> "Now when Jesus had heard that John was cast into prison, he departed into Galilee . . . From that time Jesus began to preach, and to say, Repent: for the kingdom of heaven is at hand" (Mathew 4:12-17).

At the time of Christ, almost everyone was eagerly waiting for the Kingdom of heaven to come. In spite of the many separatist groups in Palestine with divers understanding and opinions about the Kingdom, they all had one common expectation: the Messiah will come and deliver them from the hateful Romans and set up the physical Davidic throne as prophesied.

And so, when Jesus appeared on the stage announcing the Kingdom, people thronged to hear and to be with Him. In one of His opening addresses, for example, Jesus identified Himself with the prophecy of the prophet Isaiah saying:

> "This day is this scripture fulfilled in your ears" (Luke 4:21).

The atmosphere was charged following this statement and the eyes of all were fastened on Him as they "wondered at the gracious words which proceeded out of his mouth." For the skeptic and unbelieving they could not come to terms with the carpenter's Son being the expected King and Messiah and they were much offended.

In quoting the prophet Isaiah, Jesus intentionally left out a significant part of his prophesy: "to proclaim . . . the day of vengeance of our God" (Isaiah 61:1). But, this was because this portion has to do with His Second Advent.

Jesus has already come and is at the moment preparing a people for His Kingdom through His Spirit and His disciples. He would come the second time to reign.

One day, a Jewish leader came to Jesus by night and this is what followed:

> "There was a man of the Pharisees, named Nicodemus, a ruler of the Jews:

Chapter 14: His Teachings

> The same came to Jesus by night, and said unto him, Rabbi, we know that thou art a teacher come from God: for no man can do these miracles that thou doest, except God be with him.
>
> Jesus answered and said unto him, Verily, verily, I say unto thee, Except a man be born again, he cannot see the kingdom of God.
>
> Nicodemus saith unto him, How can a man be born when he is old? can he enter the second time into his mother's womb, and be born?
>
> Jesus answered, Verily, verily, I say unto thee, Except a man be born of water and of the Spirit, he cannot enter into the kingdom of God" (John 3:1-5; cf. Mark 10:17-30).

New men make new society; therefore, all must be made new if all must enter into the new heaven and new earth. The primary meaning of the phrase "Kingdom of God" is "God's sovereign rule."

The Kingdom of God is both the rule of God and the dwelling place of God. It is also the home of the Holy angels and the saints of God. To inherit eternal life is to be saved and to be saved is to be a citizen of the kingdom of Christ and of God.

Unregenerate man is generally rebellious and cannot accept the rule of God and neither can he enter the Kingdom of heaven. It is impossible for the fallen man or the unregenerate to please God; therefore, every man must be saved or born again to live as God intended.

The Jews at Jesus time were concerned about the rule of Rome, but Jesus was concerned about their rebellion to the rule of God. He was concerned about their sin and sins. This is the reason why even to date the cross is a rock of offense to the Jew and foolishness to the Gentile.

Israel dreamed of an earthly utopia. They hoped for a material prosperity, a world of provision in profusion, but had no room for the moral requirements preached by both John and Jesus Christ. True, a future, historical and visible kingdom as promised to King David is to be expected; but first, Israel and the nations must accept a spiritual kingdom with such entry requirements through the hope-for-ruler (Messiah).

This explains why they were not moved by the death of the greatest prophet of their time John the Baptist who is the epitome of the Old Testament prophets and even went on to crucify their King and Messiah.

Caiaphas being the high priest for the year correctly prophesied that Jesus should die for the nation, but this was politically assumed (John 11:50). It is sad to say, even today, Israel is still asleep. The blindness which in part has happened to them will remain until the time of the Gentiles is over according to the Scriptures:

> "For I would not, brethren, that ye should be ignorant of this mystery, lest ye should be wise in your own conceits; that blindness in part is happened to Israel, until the fulness of the Gentiles be come in.
>
> And so all Israel shall be saved: as it is written, There shall come out of Sion the Deliverer, and shall turn away ungodliness from Jacob:
>
> For this is my covenant unto them, when I shall take away their sins" (Romans 11:25-27).

Upon the implicit rejection of the King and the kingdom, Jesus announced the turning-point; "I will build my Church." His church at the moment is made up of both Jews and Gentiles on earth and in heaven. For now His Church exists in its spiritual form and will continue to do so till He returns to set up the "throne of David" and the "house of Jacob:"

> "He shall be great, and shall be called the Son of the Highest: and the Lord God shall give unto him the throne of his father David:

Chapter 14: His Teachings

And he shall reign over the house of Jacob for ever; and of his kingdom there shall be no end" (Luke 1:32-33).

The fact that we have His First Advent means we shall also have His Second Advent. When Jesus Christ the King returns, repented Israel shall say, "Blessed is he that cometh in the name of the Lord.

The hope-for ruler of Israel shall be realized; and all the Old Testament prophecies fulfilled and completed:

"Behold, your house is left unto you desolate: and verily I say unto you, Ye shall not see me, until the time come when ye shall say, Blessed is he that cometh in the name of the Lord" (Luke 13:35).

The Kingdom has a future as well as a present; it has an already and not yet. For example, the kingdom is already with all who are spiritually born again, but the King of kings and Lord of Lords, who will mark an end of the worldly systems and usher in a new world order has not yet returned:

"And there shall be no more curse: but the throne of God and of the Lamb shall be in it; and his servants shall serve him: And they shall see his face; and his name shall be in their foreheads.

And there shall be no night there; and they need no candle, neither light of the sun; for the Lord God giveth them light: and they shall reign for ever and ever.

And he said unto me, these sayings are faithful and true: and the Lord God of the holy prophets sent his angel to shew unto his servants the things which must shortly be done. Behold, I come quickly: blessed is he that keepeth the sayings of the prophecy of this book" (Revelations 22:3-7).

The church is not the Kingdom, but it is within the Kingdom. The vocation of every disciple of Jesus Christ is to preach and teach the good news of the Kingdom:

> "Go ye therefore, and teach all nations, baptizing them in the name of the Father, and of the Son, and of the Holy Ghost.
>
> Teaching them to observe all things whatsoever I have commanded you: and, lo, I am with you always, even unto the end of the world. Amen" (Mathew 28:19-20).

We shall know what God is saying to each of us if we pay attention to the teachings of Jesus Christ. God the Father calls on every man to listen to His Son:

> **"This is my Son, the chosen One. Listen to Him"** (Luke 9:35; cf. Deuteronomy 6:4).

Jesus Christ is the Word become flesh. The work of the Holy Spirit is to reveal Him to all who seek to know God. The Spirit of God testifies to the deity and redemption work of the Son:

> **Even the Spirit of truth, which proceedeth from the Father, he shall testify of me,"** (John 16:26).

The teachings of Jesus Christ are not empty words or the words of a braggart. His words are with power. He demonstrated His doctrine with signs, wonders and miracles:

> "And they were all amazed, insomuch that they questioned among themselves, saying, What thing is this? what new doctrine is this? for with authority commandeth he even the unclean spirits, and they do obey him" (Mark 1:27).

The teachings are the very words of God to His human creatures. Jesus Christ did not learn them from any religious institution; His hearers did testify to that saying:

> **"How knoweth this man letters, having never learned?"** (John 7:15).

Here is God's admonishing to all of us: "Harden not your hearts, as in the provocation, in the day of temptation in the wilderness."

We must all kiss Jesus the Christ with a genuine kiss if we are to escape eternal condemnation on the Day of Judgment and accountability:

"Kiss the Son, lest he be angry, and ye perish from the way, when his wrath is kindled but a little. Blessed are all they that put their trust in him" (Psalm 2:12).

Let us be doers of the word and not hearers only, deceiving ourselves. I pray none of us would be like the man who looks at his face in the mirror and forgets who he is immediately he walks away from it. If any man pays attention to His words he shall live.

Notes

Chapter 15

His Works

We know from the Gospel records that the world itself cannot contain all that Jesus said and did if each of them were to be written; therefore, I will not try to be a superman. Instead, I will be brief and short:

> "And there are also many other things which Jesus did, the which, if they should be written every one, I suppose that even the world itself could not contain the books that should be written" (John 21:25).

The four letters which come together to form the Gospels all agree that Jesus Christ was a mighty worker. He was a man who did mighty works:

> "What manner of man is this, that even the wind and the sea obey him?" (Mark 4:41).

Thousands of people gathered to hear Him: "People ran afoot thither out of all cities, and out went them, and came together unto him" (Mark 6:33; 4:41). "They were astonished with a great astonished" at His works (Mark 5:42):

> "And ran through that whole region round about, and began to carry about in beds those that were sick, where they heard he was.

> And whithersoever he entered, into villages, or cities, or country, they laid the sick in the streets, and besought him that they might touch if it were but the border of his garment: and as many as touched him were made whole" (Mark 6:55-56).

The quality of His work was beyond measure. The sick and the diseased were restored to perfect wholeness. The healings were instant, permanent and without any trace of the disease remaining. There was no trace of a failure or relapse of anyone healed:

> "And were beyond measure astonished, saying, He hath done all things well: he maketh both the deaf to hear, and the dumb to speak" (Mark 7:37).

They brought to him all who were diseased, and those that were possessed with devils. He healed many that were sick of divers' diseases, and cast out many devils. He was the miracle worker.

People thronged to Him everywhere He was found. They came to Him from all over the world. He was the fulfillment of the prophecy of Isaiah chapter 53:

> "But he was wounded for our transgressions, he was bruised for our iniquities: the chastisement of our peace was upon him; and with his stripes we are healed" (Isaiah 53:5).

Jesus "Himself took our infirmities and bare sicknesses" (Mathew 8:7). He did not heal everybody who was sick, but when healing or a miracle was essential, He was ready for it.

He refused none that sought His help. His method of healing was simple. He healed simply by His spoken word in most cases. He also healed by remote control – from afar:

> The centurion answered and said, Lord, I am not worthy that thou shouldest come under my roof: but speak the word only, and my servant shall be healed" (Mathew 8:8).

Chapter 15: His Works

He was a master in every aspect of human ailment. Sometimes, He spoke and touched the sick and other times the sick touched Him. Either way the sick were healed completely.

Time and space is not on my side to elaborate on every single work of Jesus Christ, but I can simplify it by tabulating a few for you:

1. Lepers were cleansed.
2. Those suffering from palsies were healed.
3. Those suffering from fever like Peter's mother-in-law.
4. He stilled the storm.
5. Demoniacs were freed and healed.
6. Those suffering from hemorrhages were healed.
7. The blind and even the born blind received their sight.
8. The crippled, paralytics and lamed were healed.
9. The dead were raised back to life.
10. The dumb spoke with vivid clarity.
11. Deaf ears were opened.
12. He turned water into wine.
13. Walked on the sea.
14. Fed thousands with just few loaves and fishes.
15. Draught of fishes caught at his word.
16. Withered hand restored.
17. Impotent healed.
18. Dropsy healed.
19. Malchus' ear restored.
20. Coin found in the belly of a fish at His word.
21. All sick people that were taken with divers disease and torments:

> "And Jesus went about all Galilee, teaching in their synagogues, and preaching the gospel of the kingdom, and healing all manner of sickness and all manner of disease among the people.
>
> And his fame went throughout all Syria: and they brought unto him all sick people that were taken with divers diseases and torments, and those which were possessed with devils, and those which were lunatick, and those that had the palsy; and he healed them" (Mathew 4:23-24).

Jesus Christ said all the works He did were the works the Father had given Him to finish. They were not His works, but that of the Father.

Further, they were not works prompted by His feelings, emotions or sympathy. Further still, they were not products of His will (John 5:36).

Remember, He said He did not come to earth to do His own will, but the will of the Father:

> "But I have greater witness than that of John: for the works which the Father hath given me to finish, the same works that I do, bear witness of me, that the Father hath sent me" (John 5:36).

Before I close this chapter, I would like to comment on the uniqueness peculiar to the work Jesus Christ did and which differentiates His works from some of what we see being done in His name today.

Jesus Christ never did anything for show and neither did He do any miracle or perform acts of healing for His personal aggrandizement.

He never paraded His works to win adherents or win any popular support of His deity or manhood. Whatever he did and said was purely for the glory of God:

> "The Pharisees also with the Sadducees came, and tempting desired him that he would shew them a sign from heav-

en. He answered and said unto them, When it is evening, ye say, It will be fair weather: for the sky is red.

And in the morning, It will be foul weather to day: for the sky is red and lowering. O ye hypocrites, ye can discern the face of the sky; but can ye not discern the signs of the times?

A wicked and adulterous generation seeketh after a sign; and there shall no sign be given unto it, but the sign of the prophet Jonas. And he left them, and departed" (Mathew 16:4:1-4; cf. 4:6).

There were times He would strictly warn those healed not to publish their miracle healing or what He has been doing for them. The healings were not for sale or advertisement. Jesus never used healing as a way to popularize Himself:

"And he charged them straitly that no man should know it; and commanded that something should be given her to eat" (Mark 5:43; 9:9).

His miracle works were the insignia of His Messianic mission. They were God's approval of His person and mission. The miracle works of the only Son of God is a testimony and proof of who He is.

Read two of such statements:

"Jesus answered them, I told you, and ye believe not: the works that I do in my Father's name, they bear witness of me" (John 10:25; cf. verses 37,38).

"Believest thou not that I am in the Father, and the Father in me? the words that I speak unto you I speak not of myself: but the Father that dwelleth in me, he doeth the works.

Believe me that I am in the Father, and the Father in me: or else believe me for the very works' sake.

> **Verily, verily, I say unto you, He that believeth on me, the works that I do shall he do also; and greater works than these shall he do; because I go unto my Father" (John 14:10-12).**

As a matter of fact, miracles such as Jesus did and those of His faithful apostles and disciples are expressions of Divine power.

Miracle works are marvels of judgment against sin, grace for salvation through the blood of Jesus, mercy for the consequences of sin, and the power of God over the forces of darkness:

> **"Ye men of Israel, hear these words; Jesus of Nazareth, a man approved of God among you by miracles and wonders and signs, which God did by him in the midst of you, as ye yourselves also know" (Acts 2:22).**

Unbelief is a great hindrance to miracle works (Mark 6:5-6; Acts 14:3). "There is no belief that is not lived and no unbelief that is not lived." (All major heresies major in denying the works and words of Jesus the Christ).

Throughout history, God has used miracle works as evidence of His presence and even in some cases to authenticate the credentials of His messengers. A typical New Testament example is the calling of an apostle.

Anyone who says or is called an apostle of Jesus Christ must have this proof:

> **"Truly the signs of an apostle were wrought among you in all patience, in signs, and wonders, and mighty deeds" (2 Corinthians 12:12).**

Jesus and the apostles are not alone in this, even to the present; God still confirms His word through His faithful messengers. The Lord works with all those He calls and sends out to preach the Gospel:

> **"And they went forth, and preached every where, the Lord working with them, and confirming the word with signs following. Amen" (Mark 16:20).**

Chapter 15: His Works

Because He is on the throne, His disciples can use His name to destroy all the damage done by sin. What we need as His church to win the world is not great ideas, titles, more money and Christian schools, but faith that produces works:

> "Verily, verily, I say unto you, He that believeth on me, the works that I do shall he do also; and greater works than these shall he do; because I go unto my Father" (John 14:12).

The most powerful unit of measurement of God under the New Covenant is the resurrection of Jesus Christ:

> "And what is the exceeding greatness of his power to us-ward who believe, according to the working of his mighty power,
>
> Which he wrought in Christ, when he raised him from the dead, and set him at his own right hand in the heavenly places,
>
> Far above all principality, and power, and might, and dominion, and every name that is named, not only in this world, but also in that which is to come" (Ephesians 1:19-21).

It supersedes that of the Old Testament unit of measurement which was the exodus under Moses:

> "In all the signs and the wonders, which the LORD sent him to do in the land of Egypt to Pharaoh, and to all his servants, and to all his land (Deuteronomy 34:11; cf. Deuteronomy 26:8; Psalm 78:43; Micah 7:15)

The name Jesus or Jesus Christ is the power of God unto salvation to all who choose to believe. In his name, God permits mighty wonders, signs and acts of miracles to demonstrate the presence of the King and the kingdom.

The power of God is in the name of Jesus or is the name of Jesus Christ. The Spirit who is the executive power of the Godhead lives in the holy name of Jesus bodily:

"And he said unto them, Go ye into all the world, and preach the gospel to every creature. He that believeth and is baptized shall be saved; but he that believeth not shall be damned.

And these signs shall follow them that believe; In my name shall they cast out devils; they shall speak with new tongues" (Mark 16:15-17).

"No man can do the miracles Jesus did except God be with him" (John 3:2). Jesus was a man approved of God by miracles and signs and wonders:

"God anointed Jesus of Nazareth with the Holy Ghost and with power: who went about doing good, and healing all that were oppressed of the devil; for God was with him" (Acts 10:38).

He was on earth on a mission – to execute the purpose of God. To make the one and only true God known to lost and depraved humanity. To show to man obedience to God is the better way of life (John 11:4).

In summary: What Jesus Christ did proved who He was. What is being done through His name proves He is alive. He rose from the dead to give every human being eternal life. Every man must die in Christ and rise to a new man. Because He lives forever, every man in Him would live forever.

Chapter 16

CHRIST AND HIS CHURCH

This book would be incomplete without a chapter on the unique relationship that exists between Jesus Christ and His church which He calls His body and bride.

Jesus said He came to the earth to bear witness to the truth of His kingship. He came the first time to call and make a people for the kingdom and He is coming the second time to rule and reign:

Pilate therefore said unto him, Art thou a king then? Jesus answered, Thou sayest that I am a king. To this end was I born, and for this cause came I into the world, that I should bear witness unto the truth. Every one that is of the truth heareth my voice" (Mathew 18:37).

No king exists without a kingdom. It is, therefore, appropriate that His priority is to call and prepare a people for the Kingdom.

Jesus knew very well that God had given Him the kingdom, and therefore, came to earth to share the prosperity of His kingdom with mankind:

"And I appoint unto you a kingdom, as my Father hath appointed unto me" (Luke 22:29).

Here is what the prophet Daniel had to say about the Messianic Kingdom:

> "And in the days of these kings shall the God of heaven set up a kingdom, which shall never be destroyed: and the kingdom shall not be left to other people, but it shall break in pieces and consume all these kingdoms, and it shall stand for ever" (Daniel 2:44; cf. 7:24).

At the heart of Jesus' doctrine is the arrival of the kingdom which He said is initiated by His presence:

> "From that time Jesus began to preach, and to say, Repent: for the kingdom of heaven is at hand" (Mathew 4:17).

First, Jesus Christ presented the Kingdom to the natural seeds of Abraham, but they rejected it. Their final words were: "We would not have this man reign over us." Then, Jesus announced His next plan of action – to build His church. Through the church God's eternal plan would be fulfilled. From the ashes of the unbelief of the Jewish community, God would raise believers from all nations who would embrace the King and the Kingdom.

"O the depth of the riches both of the wisdom and the knowledge of God! How unsearchable are his judgments, and his ways past finding" (Romans 11:33). The activities of man cannot change the eternal purpose of God. If we are unfaithful, God remains faithful.

Truly, "who have known the mind of God? Or have been his counselor?" Paul, a later apostle, received from the Lord Jesus this commission:

> "And he (Jesus) said unto me, depart: For I will send you far hence unto the Gentiles" (Acts 22:21; cf. Acts 28:28).

Jesus came to His own world, but His world rejected Him. He came to the natural brethren but they rejected Him. The Messiah they so long awaited became to them the rock of offense and a stumbling stone because of unbelief. They failed to recognize Jesus as the expected Messiah-King (cf. Mathew 13:14; Mark 4:12; Luke 8:10; John 12:40).

Chapter 16: Jesus Christ and His Church

Further, Israel failed to live up to the purpose of their calling and their mission as the apostolic people of God. As a result, God gave them over to the spirit of slumber "until the times of the fullness of the Gentiles is come or fulfilled" (cf. Luke 21:24; Romans 11:25).

Now, with the church God can call out and prepare a people for Himself from all nations unto His name and into His kingdom:

> "He came to that which belonged to Him [to His own-- His domain, creation, things, world], and they who were His own did not receive Him and did not welcome Him.
>
> But to as many as did receive and welcome Him, He gave the authority (power, privilege, right) to become the children of God, that is, to those who believe in (adhere to, trust in, and rely on) His name" (John 1:11-12).

Jesus announced the formation of a "new community" of elected individuals – a people who are called out of the world to be His very own; a people who would not only minister to Him, but also be His witnesses – Jews, Gentiles, barbarians, nobles, rich and poor:

> "But ye are a chosen generation, a royal priesthood, an holy nation, a peculiar people; that ye should shew forth the praises of him who hath called you out of darkness into his marvellous light" (1 Peter 2:9).

Peter's confession was to be the foundation for His church. Peter acknowledges His deity (Lordship) saying: "Thou art the Christ, the Son of the living God."

> "And I say also unto thee, That thou art Peter, and upon this rock I will build my church; and the gates of hell shall not prevail against it" (Mathew 16:18).

Jesus played the word "huge rock," which in Greek is "Petros" against the name Peter which is means a stone and in Greek "Petra" (cf. John 1:42).

To paraphrase what Jesus said: "You are Petras, but on these Petros I will build my Church." You are a stone but on these rock or confession I will build my church. Jesus Christ Himself is the rock or the foundation on which His church is to be built:

"For other foundation can no man lay than that is laid, which is Jesus Christ" (1 Corinthians 3:11).

From the beginning, Jesus Christ chose twelve disciples through whom to propagate His kingdom agenda. These men later became known as the twelve apostles. These twelve were a counterpart and superior to the twelve tribes of Israel:

"And I appoint unto you a kingdom, as my Father hath appointed unto me; That ye may eat and drink at my table in my kingdom, and sit on thrones judging the twelve tribes of Israel" (Mathew 22:29-30).

Jesus Christ is superior to Moses; likewise, His new community or church is superior to the community of God's people under Moses. These twelve, Jesus said, would someday join Him to judge the twelve tribes of Israel:

"And Jesus said unto them, Verily I say unto you, That ye which have followed me, in the regeneration when the Son of man shall sit in the throne of his glory, ye also shall sit upon twelve thrones, judging the twelve tribes of Israel" (Mathew 19:28).

Graciously, Jesus Christ included His chosen, called and ordained apostles and prophets to the foundation of His church; He Himself being the cornerstone:

"And are built upon the foundation of the apostles and prophets, Jesus Christ himself being the chief corner stone" (Ephesians 2:20; cf. Revelation 21:14).

The church is the spiritual organism with Jesus Christ as the head. It is the mystic body and the bride of Christ. Literally, the word "church," means "a chosen or called out assembly." But, Jesus took it and gave it a weightier meaning when He used it

Chapter 16: Jesus Christ and His Church

for His "new people" in contradistinction to Israel the church which was in the wilderness (Acts 7:38).

Further, the word "church" is applicable essentially to people and never to a building in which public worship is conducted. In its broadest sense it is used to describe "the company of the faithful in Christ" all over the world.

Further still, it is used to denote the assemblies of the scattered groups of those blood-redeemed and Spirit-born human beings in a particular region and state, a body of Christians dwelling in the same immediate locality or even a small group of Christians meeting together in a house for worship and edification.

Entrance into the church and membership is solely based upon a relationship with Jesus Christ. This relationship can only be established by an acknowledgment of His deity through His Spirit. In other words, the church is made up of true believers who acknowledge the deity of Jesus Christ as Peter did:

"That if thou shalt confess with thy mouth the Lord Jesus, and shalt believe in thine heart that God hath raised him from the dead, thou shalt be saved" (Romans 10:9).

Remember, the kingdom of God or heaven as already mentioned is the sphere of God's reign – the heavens and the earth with all that is in them. The universal kingdom Jesus came to establish is that which He would preside as Messiah-King in fulfillment of the promise that was made to Abraham, Moses, King David and spoken about by the prophet Daniel (cf. 2 Samuel 7:13; Jeremiah 33:17). The church, which is a spiritual organism, must not be confused with the Messianic Kingdom which is outward and material.

The church exclusively belongs to Jesus Christ. Every member of the church is purchased by His blood or death and solely belongs to Him (cf. 1 Corinthians 6:20; 1 Peter 1:18-19). The church is entered in individually, but once inside, you become a part of multitude of redeemed people which no man can count. Community, as opposed to individual or personal religion is what the church stands for.

Here is an example of the community nature of the church:

"Moreover if thy brother shall trespass against thee, go and tell him his fault between thee and him alone: if he shall hear thee, thou hast gained thy brother.

But if he will not hear thee, then take with thee one or two more, that in the mouth of two or three witnesses every word may be established.

And if he shall neglect to hear them, tell it unto the church: but if he neglect to hear the church, let him be unto thee as an heathen man and a publican" (Mathew 18:15-17).

Again, its community nature is emphasized by the admonishment in the book to the Hebrews 10:25, which command members of the church, "not to forsake the assembling of themselves together."

Beware, this "assembling of themselves" does not mean denomination or non-denominationalism, which more often than not, thrives by dividing the body of Christ; it is neither an external organization or hierarchical system. The church is Spiritual, autonomous, and local.

Simply, it is "where two or three are gathered together in my name, there am I in the midst of them" (Mathew 18:20). Only if we would allow the Holy Spirit to be the head of His church; if we would allow Him to choose His own pastors and leaders; if we would let the Great Shepherd lead His sheep to where He wants them to go and be nourished, what a powerful, dynamic and flawless church that would pervade the earth!

Again, forget about all the names of individuals on church registers and books purporting to be Christians or heaven bound. Salvation is private and personal (only those who are saved can testify to the surety of their salvation).

Clearly, Jesus Christ laid out some of the benefits of the oneness, togetherness and freedom of His community of new people in the following verses:

> "Again I say unto you, that if two of you shall agree on earth as touching any thing that they shall ask, it shall be done for them of my Father which is in heaven. For where two or three are gathered together in my name, there am I in the midst of them" (Mathew 18:19-20).

Jesus Christ gave the keys of the kingdom of heaven (not the church) to Peter and the apostles telling them to go into all the nations and preach the all-inclusive-Gospel of the kingdom to every creature (Mathew 16; 28).

The keys are the good news of Gospel or the kingdom. The Gospel is the "power of God unto salvation to every one that believeth (cf. Romans 1:16):

> "The Spirit of the Lord is upon me, because he hath anointed me to preach the gospel to the poor; he hath sent me to heal the brokenhearted, to preach deliverance to the captives, and recovering of sight to the blind, to set at liberty them that are bruised, to preach the acceptable year of the Lord" (Luke 4:18-19).

Peter and the rest of the apostles entered the kingdom by their faith in Jesus Christ, and so shall everyone who hears and believes the Gospel as it is preached; first, by the apostles and the prophets, and then by all disciples till He returns (Romans 3:22).

The church has never ended since it began. Its continuation is not dependent upon one man, family, one institution or agency. "A man may be faithful for a while and yet eventually proved barren. In this case, God is never without collateral lines."

Jesus Christ would always be the head of His church and this position; He would never assign to anyone. He Himself lives on forever. He directs, control, guides and governs His church through the agency of his Spirit:

> "And he is the head of the body, the church: who is the beginning, the firstborn from the dead; that in all things he might have the preeminence" (Colossians 1:18).

He works and speaks by the Holy Spirit and would continue to do so until He physically returns for His church. The Spirit is the only person who can save sinners from sin in Christ and then translate them into the kingdom which is of God and of Christ:

> **"And the Lord added to the church daily such as should be saved" (Acts 2:47).**

> **"God also bearing them witness, both with signs and wonders, and with divers miracles, and gifts of the Holy Ghost, according to his own will?" (Hebrews 2:4; cf. Mark 16:20).**

It is essential for the church of Jesus Christ to recognize the role and the irreplaceable position of the Spirit within her.

Before His departure, Jesus warned His disciples not to depart from Jerusalem, or start the work of evangelism and ministry in His name until they receive the promise of the Father; the Holy Spirit:

> **"But ye shall receive power, after that the Holy Ghost is come upon you: and ye shall be witnesses unto me both in Jerusalem, and in all Judaea, and in Samaria, and unto the uttermost part of the earth" (Acts 1:8; Luke 24:49; John 16).**

It is unthinkable to believe that such a universal community and a priceless mission would be handed over to Peter and the apostles.

Be aware that just a few minutes after Peter confessed Jesus Christ as Lord, he was rebuked as having the mind of the devil (Mathew 16:21-23). Jesus Christ did not hand over His church to Peter or to any of the apostles as some have come to believe.

Only God can testify of God and if the disciples or apostles are to testify of the man who is fully God and fully man then it is the Spirit of God who can enable them to do so. Jesus is always working with His church.

The Holy Spirit was in-charge even when Jesus was on earth and would continue to do so even now that He is on the throne in heaven to represent His Church before the Father:

"But when the Comforter is come, whom I will send unto you from the Father, even the Spirit of truth, which proceedeth from the Father, he shall testify of me: And ye also shall bear witness, because ye have been with me from the beginning" (John 15:26-27).

The Holy Spirit possesses the church and not the church possessing the Spirit. The Spirit of Christ is her life and power.

Any group of people or assembly that gathers together in His name and where the Spirit is absent is not of Christ or gathered in His name. Jesus Christ presence on earth and Lordship over His body is known by the presence of the Holy Spirit.

The reason the church of Jesus Christ, which was born with such power and glory, is so weak and beggarly is because man is in control instead of the Spirit. Christians were first called "the way" (Acts 9:2; 19:9; 22:4; 24:14). They were the "way showers," and led the way in morals and obedience to God.

Today, one wonders if what we see and call Christianity or Christians is the church. The idea so often trotted forth is that Christianity is whatever you happen to make it. What we see and hear is far removed from what prompted the unbelieving people in Antioch to give the disciples of Jesus Christ the nick name, "Christian" (cf. Acts 11:26). I must confess the term "Christian nation" is a misnomer.

Again, I would not hesitate to say that, if "Christianity," by definition is "the church," then it is rather the field of wheat and tare. It is the community that is replete of wheat and tares and will be separated on the Day of Judgment:

"Let both grow together until the harvest: and in the time of harvest I will say to the reapers, Gather ye together first the tares, and bind them in bundles to burn them:

but gather the wheat into my barn" (Mathew 13:30; cf. verse 25-29)

The difference between the wheat and the tares is that the wheat lives to please God and the tares live to please oneself, and this is what you find in Christianity. It is the self-made, self-righteous, religious and hypocritical obedience to God in which case the tares is the visible Christian community.

The church, on the other hand, is highly profitable to the Lord and are kept and preserved by Him. It is the invisible church which is on earth purposely to do the will of God. Christianity would only be the church if her life and mission is the same as that of Jesus Christ – a community that is chosen, called, born and indwelt by God.

They are God's family and sheep. He calls them individually by name and they follow Him:

"My sheep hear my voice, and I know them, and they follow me. And I give unto them eternal life; and they shall never perish, neither shall any man pluck them out of my hand.

My Father, which gave them me, is greater than all; and no man is able to pluck them out of my Father's hand. I and my Father are one" (John 10:27-30).

"The sheep hear his voice: and he calleth his own sheep by name, and leadeth them out. And when he putteth forth his own sheep, he goeth before them, and the sheep follow him: for they know his voice.

And a stranger will they not follow, but will flee from him: for they know not the voice of strangers" (John 10:4; cf. verses 16).

The church as a living organism is directly connected to the living Christ and Savior. The saying, "God has no grandchildren" may be true of the church. Everyone in the church is a son and must live like the Son of God (cf. John 1:12).

Chapter 16: Jesus Christ and His Church

The oil with which the church is anointed is the same Jesus Christ was anointed with, namely the Holy Spirit (cf. 1 Corinthians 1:21-22). Every born again member of the church is indwelt by the Holy Spirit. This is or should be the meaning behind the name "Christian," for believers are "little Christ," and "little anointed ones."

Jesus said He would build His church and the gates of hell shall not prevail against it. The gates of hell, which holds God's elected prisoners, shall be overcome, and God's people shall be freed by the power of the Gospel.

All religion is self-made or man-made. They are man's own invention or effort to seek and to please God. It is man, again, building the tower of Babel; it is nothing, but confusion. It is self righteousness – man sewing again the fig leaves to cover his nakedness and shame and man's self-effort to bridge his estrangement from God.

The Church of Jesus Christ pre-dates history. Jesus did not set it up out of frustration, and neither is it an afterthought. Members were chosen before the foundation of the world.

God by His foreknowledge had long time ago overruled the Jewish rejection of the King without any infringement to their will or overriding their will. The church was chosen before history but called in history:

"According as he hath chosen us in him before the foundation of the world, that we should be holy and without blame before him in love" (Ephesians 1:4; Romans 8:29-30).

The call of the church is to be holy and blameless before God as already mentioned. The church is the bride and the body of Christ – distinct but inseparable. The head is holy and so is or should be the body. The church is in the world, but not of the world.

Further, on earth, the Church is parochial or a sojourner. Born again by God, members of the church are not citizens of the earth. They are heavenly minded, but not earthly useless:

"If ye then be risen with Christ, seek those things which are above, where Christ sitteth on the right hand of God. Set your affection on things above, not on things on the earth" (Colossians 3:1-2).

Again, the church is not a reformed world, but the body of individuals hand picked by God to inherit the world to come. Every member of the church is a son, a bride, and a temple of God.

There are no classifications whatsoever within her:

"There is neither Jew nor Greek, there is neither bond nor free, there is neither male nor female: for ye are all one in Christ Jesus" (Galatians 3:28).

Jesus said, "My kingdom is not of this world. There is only one head, who is Christ, and the church which is His body. The unity of the kingdom can be clearly seen in prayer Jesus prayed before His departure. Carefully consider it:

"These words spake Jesus, and lifted up his eyes to heaven, and said, Father, the hour is come; glorify thy Son, that thy Son also may glorify thee: As thou hast given him power over all flesh, that he should give eternal life to as many as thou hast given him.

And this is life eternal, that they might know thee the only true God, and Jesus Christ, whom thou hast sent. I have glorified thee on the earth: I have finished the work which thou gavest me to do.

And now, O Father, glorify thou me with thine own self with the glory which I had with thee before the world was. I have manifested thy name unto the men which thou gavest me out of the world: thine they were, and thou gavest them me; and they have kept thy word.

Now they have known that all things whatsoever thou hast given me are of thee. For I have given unto them the words which thou gavest me; and they have received them, and have known surely that I came out from thee, and they have believed that thou didst send me.

I pray for them: I pray not for the world, but for them which thou hast given me; for they are thine. And all mine are thine, and thine are mine; and I am glorified in them.

And now I am no more in the world, but these are in the world, and I come to thee. Holy Father, keep through thine own name those whom thou hast given me, that they may be one, as we are.

While I was with them in the world, I kept them in thy name: those that thou gavest me I have kept, and none of them is lost, but the son of perdition; that the scripture might be fulfilled.

And now come I to thee; and these things I speak in the world, that they might have my joy fulfilled in themselves. I have given them thy word; and the world hath hated them, because they are not of the world, even as I am not of the world.

I pray not that thou shouldest take them out of the world, but that thou shouldest keep them from the evil. They are not of the world, even as I am not of the world. Sanctify them through thy truth: thy word is truth.

As thou hast sent me into the world, even so have I also sent them into the world. And for their sakes I sanctify myself, that they also might be sanctified through the truth.

Neither pray I for these alone, but for them also which shall believe on me through their word" (John 17:1-20).

The Church is a community of redeemed individuals whose vocation is to be the salt and the light of the world. The church, acting as the light of the world, would expose and hinder ignorance or darkness. Further, the church, acting as the salt of the earth, would reveal, hold back, or destroy unbelief and the lies of Satan.

The one and only true God is made manifest in and through the church to a world that does not know Him or recognize Him as God. Eternal life for every man is to know God and His Son Jesus Christ whom He has made the propitiation for all sins:

"And this is life eternal, that they might know thee the only true God, and Jesus Christ, whom thou hast sent" (John 17:3; cf. 1 John 5:20).

There are ways by which the church can be known by the world. Briefly, here are a few of them:

1. Unity and oneness – " That they all may be one, [just] as You, Father, are in Me and I in You, that they also may be one in Us, so that the world may believe and be convinced that You have sent Me" (John 17:21 cf. verse 23).

2. By their fruit or conduct – "Ye shall know them by their fruits. Do men gather grapes of thorns, or figs of thistles? Wherefore by their fruits ye shall know them" (Mathew 7:16, 20).

3. Separation from the world – "If ye were of the world, the world would love his own: but because ye are not of the world, but I have chosen you out of the world, therefore the world hateth you" (John 15:19; cf. 1 Corinthians 5:20).

4. Holiness – "According as he hath chosen us in him before the foundation of the world, that we should be holy and without blame before him in love" (Ephesians 1:4).

5. Mission as ambassadors for Christ – "Now then we are ambassadors for Christ, as though God did beseech you

Chapter 16: Jesus Christ and His Church

by us: we pray you in Christ's stead, be ye reconciled to God" (2 Corinthians 5:20).

6. Heavenly mindedness – "If ye then be risen with Christ, seek those things which are above, where Christ sitteth on the right hand of God. Set your affection on things above, not on things on the earth. For ye are dead, and your life is hid with Christ in God" (Colossians 3:1-3; 2 Peter 3).

7. Bond of love within her – "A new commandment I give unto you, that ye love one another; as I have loved you, that ye also love one another. By this shall all men know that ye are my disciples, if ye have love one to another" (John 13:34-35).

As a living organism, the Spirit is the life and light within church. The Spirit serves as the ligament linking together each member. Individually, the church is anyone in whom the Spirit or Jesus dwells. Collectively, the church is the body with many parts in Christ and indwelt by God – the household of faith (cf. Galatians 6:10).

Again, the church is the new community of God where the Spirit dwells and leads. They are a people of faith; faith obeys. A life of obedience to God is an indication of the Spirit's presence. It is a sign of belonging to God's family. It does not bring you into the family, but it is what family members do.

Every work by the church, within and without should or must be Spirit initiated and Spirit wrought without exception. Every turn and twist in the church's doings is or should be directed by Him.

There is a difference between working for the Lord and the Lord asking you to do work or do something for Him. No work is worth doing if it is not God initiated. The simple rule is: If God has not asked you to do something for Him do not create one by yourself.

There is a common mission for the church; witnessing or testifying for Christ is the duty of every born again member of the church. Every child of God is anointed from the moment of salvation to preach the Gospel to their neighbor or family. This duty requires no human endorsement, ordination, or letters of recommendation.

However, callings and gifting such as the five-fold ministry are only for those selected or chosen by the Holy Spirit within the body. No institution, organization, or local congregants can ordain, confer, or produce them. It is the prerogative of the Lord Jesus Christ Himself.

They are already ordained and equipped for the job by virtue of their divine calling. This is not to say these do not need training, surely they do, but as to whether they need further ordination by men is a million questions we must all answer:

"And he gave some, apostles; and some, prophets; and some, evangelists; and some, pastors and teachers" (Ephesians 4:11).

God employs His own workers. Every minister within the church must be handpicked by the Lord without exception. To be good stewards of the great commission, every member of the church is asked to be a student of the Bible.

Each of us is called upon to personally and collectively to study the Bible. We must meditate on the word of God day and night:

"Study to shew thyself approved unto God, a workman that needeth not to be ashamed, rightly dividing the word of truth" (2 Timothy 2:15).

Every member of the body of Christ is gifted from the moment of salvation by the indwelling Spirit of God. God has a special gift for every one that He brings into the kingdom of Christ.

You may not know your gift, but that does not mean you do not have one or even more. Each of us has some gift(s) for the edification of the body of Christ:

"But the manifestation of the Spirit is given to every man to profit withal" (1 Corinthians 12:7).

Because of the nature and the holy vocation of the church, members are to spur each other to do good works. Unbridled tongue and all forms of sin must not be encouraged within her. All must watch and pray, lest they enter into temptation and fail.

Pollutions from the world must not be allowed to breed within the church. Tares must be exposed. Where we are unable to remove them, we must stay away: "A little leaven leaveneth the whole lump" (Galatians 5:9; cf. verse 6).

Achan, Ananias and Sapphira must not be allowed into the church. The church must not segregate from the world but from anyone within the church who openly puts the name of the Lord Jesus Christ to shame by way of conduct:

> **"Yet not altogether with the fornicators of this world, or with the covetous, or extortioners, or with idolaters; for then must ye needs go out of the world.**
>
> **But now I have written unto you not to keep company, if any man that is called a brother be a fornicator, or covetous, or an idolator, or a railer, or a drunkard, or an extortioner; with such an one no not to eat.**
>
> **For what have I to do to judge them also that are without? Do not ye judge them that are within?"** (1 Corinthians 5:10-12).

Jesus Christ was killed because He was different. He was separate from sinners. There was no darkness or duplicity of character in Him.

To the world, Jesus was odd and so is His church which is His body. The body should not be different from the head. The body and the head must of a necessity be of the same quality and purpose.

The church is or should reflect Jesus Christ. The goal of the Holy Spirit is to reveal Jesus in and through the church to a world that is ignorant of God and His righteousness; a world that is perishing because of sin. The church shares the same world view with her Lord: Sufferings, persecutions, purity in life and service, destination, and exaltation (Ephesians 2:6).

Remember, the church did not choose Jesus, rather, Jesus chose the church. No man can join the church by self-effort (cf. John 15:16). The church bears His name. Whatever happens to the church, good or bad, happens to Him. Wherever the church is, there He is.

The church is connected directly to the Son and to the Father by the Holy Spirit. Jesus is able to call His church brethren:

"Both he that sanctifieth and they who are sanctified are all of one: for which cause he is not ashamed to call them brethren."

The church has this injunction: "Love the Lord thy God with all thy heart, and with all thy soul, and with all thy mind, and with all thy strength: this is the first commandment.

And the second is to love thy neighbor as thyself:

"No man hath seen God at any time. If we love one another, God dwelleth in us, and his love is perfected in us" (1 John 4:12).

"In this was manifested the love of God toward us, because that God sent his only begotten Son into the world, that we might live through him.

Herein is love, not that we loved God, but that he loved us, and sent his Son to be the propitiation for our sins" (1 John 4:9-10).

He that is born of God loves his neighbor. Because "God laid down His life for us: we ought to lay down our lives for the brethren" (1 John 3:16). If we love the brethren, it shows that we have passed from death to life, but he that hates his neighbor is still in death (1 John 3:14).

Here is the "Golden rule:"

Chapter 16: Jesus Christ and His Church

"Therefore all things whatsoever ye would that men should do to you, do ye even so to them: for this is the law and the prophets" (Mathew 7:12).

In summary, there is only one church and it is that which Jesus Christ is Lord; the church that the Holy Spirit lives and freely rules. Religion is what man does, but the church is what God does. The sword of the Spirit is the word of God (Ephesians 6:17).

Notes

Chapter 17

WHAT MUST I DO?

There are many religions in the world today. Among them are: Islam, Nonreligious, Hinduism, Chinese traditional religion, Buddhism, indigenous, African Traditional, Sikhism, Juche, Spiritism, Judaism, Baha'i Jainism, Shinto, Cao Dai, Zoreastrainism, Tenrikyo and Neo-Paganism.

But honest to say, none of these can save any man from sin, death and the wrath of God to come upon the world. None offers any rational exegesis to man's present predicament of greed, irrationality and barbarism, or offer any logical explanation to the meaning of life such the purpose of our existence, the fall of man, and what happens to man hereafter.

Only the Bible, as the revealed and infallible word of God provides concrete answers to all of these and answers man's desperate cries and need. The Bible is absolutely coherent in its presentation of the truth. "Of all the books on earth, the Bible is the most wonderful in its matter and meaning and message. The whole Bible is the word of the living God.

There are many writings purported to have come from God, but none comes close to the Bible in inspiration and infallibility. Of course, many religious books do contain excerpts from the Bible, but that alone cannot make them the word of God.

Again, this is not to say that there is no wisdom at all in

them. In fact, there is wisdom in many of them, but the problem is that they are all wisdom of men. They are man's own beliefs and ideas or ideologies.

Religion is man's own effort to please and serve God or gods. They are the philosophies of men – man's search for the meaning to life. I must confess that there is nothing more damnable to man than the idea that there are many roads to the One and only True God.

Further, man's attempt to explain away sin and to eradicate it from the mind and from the world confirms man's depravity and bondage to the spirit of error. The many conflicting views of the origin of life and nature which religions of the world offer establish the Bible as the only source of truth. Truth reveals what is not true.

Information gathered from past and recent archeological excavations and discoveries has in many ways confirmed the accuracy of the Bible and the infallibility of the divine testimony.

The self-effort of the human race to be politically, academically and morally correct has all proven to be fiasco. Man seems to be caught in a dark hole filled with dirt. He cannot get himself out and neither can he make himself clean. The works of man do not produce salvation and neither can it establish a right relationship with the Creator and moral governor of the universe:

> **"Where no counsel is, the people fall: but in the multitude of counsellors there is safety" (Proverbs 11:14).**

The wages of sin are even with us in this life. Our hospitals are overflowing with the incurably diseased. Our prisons are filled with both the innocent and the guilty. Suicide is on the increase. Many people have resigned themselves to a state of hopelessness and helplessness.

Governments have failed their people. Democracy has become autocracy. Socialism, communism and capitalism are the academic man's dream and far removed from reality.

Chapter 17: What Must I Do

However, the Bible is clear that theocracy is the essence of a truly visible social order.

The world of mankind is plagued with wars, rumors of wars, economic failures, dehumanization, moral decadence, social injustice, unrest and family breakdown. The fear that the world is spiraling out of control has become a reality for many. It appears man has run out of ideas.

The sad news is that despite this gloomy state of the world and its economy man still refuses to turn to God for answers. Even though God is closer to man than ever, man is looking everywhere and even asking the devils for help with the exception of God. Increasingly, man is daily provoking God by his numerous flirtations with evil.

Yet, finding God and the salvation He alone provides has never been this easy. Today, by the grace of God, the Gospel of Jesus Christ is being preached in almost every nation under the sun. Everything about the Gospel is frank and open. There are no secret illuminations.

God in addition to Jesus has given us the Holy Spirit to teach us all things. We know all things because the Holy Spirit teaches us and not as the agnostics and new age teaches:

"But the anointing which ye have received of him abideth in you, and ye need not that any man teach you: but as the same anointing teacheth you of all things, and is truth, and is no lie, and even as it hath taught you, ye shall abide in him" (2:27; verse 20).

The Bible is being translated into many local languages and is available in almost every bookstore in the world. We are, if not already approaching the days God said the knowledge of His glory shall cover the entire world. God would not rush the end:

"For the earth shall be filled with the knowledge of the glory of the LORD, as the waters cover the sea" (Habakkuk 2:14; Isaiah 11:9).

Jesus said the end shall come after the gospel of the kingdom is preached in the entire world for a witness unto all nations and commanded that the Good news of the Gospel of salvation be preached to every creature (cf. Mathew 24). His will is that all would hear the Gospel of His Son and live.

God has given to every human being eternal life, but this life is in His Son. God wants every man to come to Him to receive life. Christ Himself is both the gate and the way and God enables men to find the gate (cf. John 14:6; 6:44).

There are many on the broad way of life and seeking to arrive in heaven by means of their own works. But, the truth is that it is only the few who receive the grace of God in Jesus Christ who are guaranteed to enter therein:

"And this is the record, that God hath given to us eternal life, and this life is in his Son. He that hath the Son hath life; and he that hath not the Son of God hath not life" (1 John 5:11-12).

The life of each and every man is too precious to be lost, destroyed or wasted. We can measure the worth of each of us by looking at how much our Creator was willing to pay for our salvation – the price being the death of His only Son.

Many people shy away from the truth of the Gospel, because their ways are evil. They are afraid to come to the light for fear that their evil deeds may get exposed. They do not want to be changed for they love the ways of evil. But, for these people I must say, "the axe is already laid at the root of the tree:"

"And this is the condemnation, that light is come into the world, and men loved darkness rather than light, because their deeds were evil. For every one that doeth evil hateth the light, neither cometh to the light, lest his deeds should be reproved" (John 3:19).

Jesus is the true light that lights the path of everyone who comes into the world (John 1:9). Every man shall stand before God to be judged at the end of the ages. Jesus Christ would decide the fate of every one of us. God has committed all judgment to Him:

> "Therefore judge nothing before the time, until the Lord come, who both will bring to light the hidden things of darkness, and will make manifest the counsels of the hearts: and then shall every man have praise of God" (1 Corinthians 4:5).

We can choose to believe now and accept Him as savior and Lord at God's expense or stay in our unbelief and face the wrath of God at the end of time ourselves. The choice is ours:

> "Whosoever believeth that Jesus is the Christ is born of God: and every one that loveth him that begat loveth him also that is begotten of him" (1 John 5:1).

God is calling every man to become His family member through the Gospel of His Son. He made us, and by the Gospel He wants each of us to return to Him. We can only accept His offer or reject it.

God is infinitely holy. He is light, and in Him is no darkness at all (1 John 1:5). To have fellowship or a right standing before Him demands that we be made holy, redeemed or born of God without exception.

We are sinners and need to be made holy to be reconciled to God. Sin is presented as slavery and sinners are slaves to sin:

> "He that committeth sin is of the devil; for the devil sinneth from the beginning. For this purpose the Son of God was manifested, that he might destroy the works of the devil.
>
> Whosoever is born of God doth not commit sin; for his seed remaineth in him: and he cannot sin, because he is born of God" (1 John 3:8-9).

He who commits sin transgresses the law. Deliverance from sin is true freedom. Christ's death is the payment for every man's release from sin and the ramifications of sin. Jesus is the propitiation for the sins of the whole world:

> "And he is the propitiation for our sins: and not for ours only, but also for the sins of the whole world" (1 John 2:2).

Redemption is not awakening to spiritual consciousness or a gradual and natural awakening of an innate consciousness of God. Redemption is outside man. It is something only God can do in Jesus Christ.

Every sinner is given grace to enter into life through faith in Christ. Enoch, the seventh from Adam, prophesied of our generation saying:

> "Behold, the Lord cometh with ten thousands of his saints, to execute judgment upon all, and to convince all that are ungodly among them of all their ungodly deeds which they have ungodly committed, and of all their hard speeches which ungodly sinners have spoken against him.
>
> These are murmurers, complainers, walking after their own lusts; and their mouth speaketh great swelling words, having men's persons in admiration because of advantage" (Jude 1:14-16).

Unbelief is the rejection of plain truth. Many people for the fear of rejection and persecution prefer tight lips. They would rather die in their current state of fear and uncertainties, even though deep within they know they must make a change. Procrastination does no man good.

Some people have voluntarily or involuntarily inherited their current religious belief from parents, or loved ones. Sheer size, age, systematic doctrine may be the reason for the stand of the many religious people.

Every religious group believes their own is the truth and best. They would rather die than change for another, which is quite understandable in view of the blindness that has befallen the human race. I must confess that Christians or church attendants are no exception to this hypocrisy and heresy.

Many denominations are quick to point fingers at others.

Chapter 17: What Must I Do

Socially, they segregate themselves as the originals, the pure or the orthodox. If Christianity means belonging to Jesus Christ, then it is already defined by the Bible. Jesus Christ, the founder and owner is the only standard and role model. He is the church's only cornerstone. His words and doctrine are its foundation and pillars.

Unlike the religions of the world, the Bible has passed the test of change. So far, it is the only book that changes people from the inside out. All others including self effort only work on the outside, they can only reform but not transform. They repair externally, but cannot make new from the inside.

The Bible is the only power of God that can transform sinners into saints. It changes the course of hell-bound sinners to heaven-bound sons of God. The salvation that God alone provides for all, deals with sin and sins, the depravity of the human heart and the consequences of sin.

New birth produces real change. It makes old people new people and new people create new societies. The unrighteous man becomes righteous through rebirth:

"A new heart also will I give you, and a new spirit will I put within you: and I will take away the stony heart out of your flesh, and I will give you an heart of flesh.

And I will put my spirit within you, and cause you to walk in my statutes, and ye shall keep my judgments, and do them" (Ezekiel 36:26-27).

Is it not strange the world seems not to know Jesus Christ? Compare all that I have shared with you so far, by the grace of God through the Spirit, concerning Jesus the Christ, and see if you can find in all the religions of the world any comparison.

See if you can find any leader that even comes close in birth, purity of life, death, resurrection, ascension, works, power and teachings of Jesus Christ – the Son of God. Can any man place on humanity the demands the life and teachings of Jesus Christ has done?

There is not a man like Jesus Christ – a man of such impeccable wholeness and holiness. Further, there is not a man who died and rose again from the dead and is alive forevermore, and in whose name diseases are healed and the dead raised back to life.

Jesus Christ bodily ascension into the heavens was witnessed by over five hundred people as he departed. Demons tremble at the mere mention of His name. Today, billions of people are saved from sins and death through the power and the salvation wrought by God through Him.

His birth has changed the calendar of the world into A.D. and B.C. He claimed to be equal with Yahweh of the Jewish-Hebrew faith, and proved His claim by miracles, signs, wonders and teachings. God publicly spoke twice from heaven claiming Him as the man in whom He is well pleased.

How can such a man be a stranger to our history and text books? How can Jesus Christ be a man that people hardly know? Is the world antagonized by Him? Or is His standard set for man too high so that He is unaccounted for?

Do not get me wrong, I am not writing these things to force Jesus down your throat; God forbid. No, this is not the intent of this book. All I am doing is relaying the truth as presented to man from the word of God. I know very well salvation is entirely the prerogative of God.

I also know that no man can, on his own, come to God, or accept Jesus Christ as Lord and Savior, except by the Holy Spirit. Unless God draws you, you cannot come to Him. But who knows, perhaps God is calling you now through this book. Any man can know the truth if so wish.

The grace of God is available to all who seek to know the truth of God's word with their whole heart. Every human being that is born into this world has the ability to know and to accept the truth when revealed. However, are we willing to accept this truth? Are we ready to live by the truth of God's word?

God created the world for Jesus Christ – His only beloved Son. When man became subject to death because of sin, and his nature became corrupt as a result, God sent His Son to the

Chapter 17: What Must I Do

cross to die, save man and then restore all things to the primer glory and beyond. Consequently, God is calling you to repent by accepting His offer. What is your response?

Truth is bitter to the taste of the ungodly. It is an enemy to the unrighteous lifestyle. Perhaps, throughout the reading of this book, you even felt some inner excitement, joy, fear, awakening, or enlightenment. Maybe you experienced some goose pimples, and the hair of your skin stood up so many times. Perhaps you were shaken or even had several temptations to lay down this book down and forget about it; I do not know.

But, there is one thing I know; God speaks to man, and this book is one of His ways of speaking to you. My prayer for you is that the heart, desire, and the feelings of Jesus Christ may become your heart, desire and feelings. May you and all those who read this book be able to say with Jesus Christ, "My food is to do the will of Him who sent me to earth" (cf. John 4:34).

Jesus Christ came purposely to earth to reconcile man to God. If you or I are the only citizens of this earth, and we fell into sin, God would still have sent His Son to die for us. Riches, honor, and the wealth of this planet cannot by any measure be compared to the prize of one human soul:

> **"I say unto you, that likewise joy shall be in heaven over one sinner that repenteth, more than over ninety and nine just persons, which need no repentance" (Luke 15:7).**

> **"Likewise, I say unto you, there is joy in the presence of the angels of God over one sinner that repenteth" (Luke 15:10).**

Finally, here is the promise of God that got me saved in 1973. If you are not sure of your salvation, you can pray the same prayer I prayed and also be saved. For God is not a man that He should lie and neither is He respecter of persons:

> **"That if thou shalt confess with thy mouth the Lord Jesus, and shalt believe in thine heart that God hath raised him from the dead, thou shalt be saved.**

> For with the heart man believeth unto righteousness; and with the mouth confession is made unto salvation.
>
> For the scripture saith, Whosoever believeth on him shall not be ashamed.
>
> For there is no difference between the Jew and the Greek: for the same Lord over all is rich unto all that call upon him.
>
> For whosoever shall call upon the name of the Lord shall be saved" (Romans 10:9-13; cf. Revelations 3:20).

The two things needed for one to receive the righteousness of God and be reconciled to Him are, belief and confession. Belief in the saving power of the risen Christ must come from the innermost (heart) part of man's being. Confession with the mouth is evidence of genuine faith in the heart (cf. Luke 12:8). "Whosoever shall call upon the name of the Lord shall be saved."

Simply, ask Jesus to be your Lord and Savior. Ask Him to forgive you all the sins you have committed against Him, and also ask Him to cleanse you from all unrighteousness. You do not need to make a list of them before God. After all, you cannot remember all of them. Simply, admit to God you are a sinner in need of salvation through Jesus Christ.

God is at the moment standing at the door of your heart waiting for you to ask Him in to come in (cf. Revelations 3:20). This confession of acceptance is all that you need to be saved. Any man who accepts Jesus Christ as Savior and Lord God lives in him or her:

> "And we know that the Son of God is come, and hath given us an understanding, that we may know him that is true, and we are in him that is true, even in his Son Jesus Christ. This is the true God, and eternal life" (1 John 5:20).

Chapter 17: What Must I Do

If you need further help you can first read my book, "Second Chance" and follow it with "Transcended life." They are available in almost all the bookstores. You can also send me an email from our web site or write me for a free copy of "A Second Chance." You are free to add a token to cover shipment.

Make every effort to grow your relationship with God through Jesus Christ: "Grow in grace, and in the knowledge of our Lord and Saviour Jesus Christ" (2 Peter 3:8). As you have received Him, so walk in Him. Be rooted and built up in him. Be established in the faith, abounding therein with thanksgiving.

In Christ dwelleth all the fullness of the Godhead bodily. And ye are complete in Him. Jesus Christ is the head of all principality and power and so be strong and bold, for the Lord thy God is with you (cf. Colossians 2).

Again, "beware lest any man spoil you through philosophy and vain deceit, after the tradition of men, after the rudiments of the world, and not after Christ. Also beware of false prophets. They appear in sheep's clothing but are in reality ravening wolves. Be mindful of the fact that the true test of a prophet is the conformity of his doctrine and life to that of scripture (1 Corinthians 14:37; Deuteronomy 13:1-5).

The good news is that He is ever ready to help all who come to Him for help:

> **"For the Father judgeth no man, but hath committed all judgment unto the Son: That all men should honour the Son, even as they honour the Father. He that honoureth not the Son honoureth not the Father which hath sent him.**
>
> **Verily, verily, I say unto you, He that heareth my word, and believeth on him that sent me, hath everlasting life, and shall not come into condemnation; but is passed from death unto life. Verily, verily, I say unto you, The hour is coming, and now is, when the dead shall hear the voice of the Son of God: and they that hear shall live.**

> For as the Father hath life in himself; so hath he given to the Son to have life in himself; And hath given him authority to execute judgment also, because he is the Son of man.
>
> Marvel not at this: for the hour is coming, in the which all that are in the graves shall hear his voice, And shall come forth; they that have done good, unto the resurrection of life; and they that have done evil, unto the resurrection of damnation" (John 5:22-27).

Jesus Christ the Son of God is fully God and fully man. Any one searching for the light need not go far, Jesus Christ is the light. He Himself is the true Light. He is the light which lightens the path of every man that cometh into the world.

Again, Jesus Christ is the wisdom of God. He is our wisdom, righteousness, sanctification, and redemption. He can help you and anyone who comes to Him for help. Every man is born diseased from the womb. As a result we all need a doctor for our spiritual bankruptcy and perversion.

Every human being needs help from Jesus Christ regardless of social, political, economic and religious standing. Jesus Christ is every man's healer and medicine.

Chapter 18

BEHOLD THE MAN

Oh what a man! I cannot wait to visibly greet Him and express my greatest gratitude. How can I stop writing on such an august man? How do I put down my pen? John was right, if all that Jesus did and said should be written, "I suppose that even the world itself could not contain the books that could be written. Amen."

The trouble is who would believe our report? How would the unaided mind accept the truth that; God, the Creator of the universe, once walked on the dusty streets of the earth purposely to save His human creatures? This truth transcends reason, but it does not contradict it.

In closing, let me return to the unifying emphasis of all that I have shared with you, namely, our Lord Jesus Christ. The Bible extracts below from the Gospel according to John is my summary to this book.

Jesus Christ had risen from the dead as He said He would. Some of the disciples went early in the morning to put some extra spices on the body, but He was not there. While wondering what had happened to Jesus' body, He appeared to two of His disciples who were on their way to a village called, Emmaus. This is the Biblical narrative:

"And, behold, two of them went that same day to a village called Emmaus, which was from Jerusalem about threescore furlongs. And they talked together of all these things which had happened.

And it came to pass, that, while they communed together and reasoned, Jesus himself drew near, and went with them. But their eyes were holden that they should not know him.

And he said unto them, what manner of communications are these that ye have one to another, as ye walk, and are sad?

And the one of them, whose name was Cleopas, answering said unto him, Art thou only a stranger in Jerusalem, and hast not known the things which are come to pass there in these days?

And he said unto them, what things? And they said unto him, Concerning Jesus of Nazareth, which was a prophet mighty in deed and word before God and all the people: And how the chief priests and our rulers delivered him to be condemned to death, and have crucified him.

But we trusted that it had been he which should have redeemed Israel: and beside all this, today is the third day since these things were done.

Yea, and certain women also of our company made us astonished, which were early at the sepulchre; And when they found not his body, they came, saying, that they had also seen a vision of angels, which said that he was alive.

And certain of them which were with us went to the sepulchre, and found it even so as the women had said: but him they saw not. Then he said unto them, O fools, and slow of heart to believe all that the prophets have spoken: Ought not Christ to have suffered these things, and to enter into his glory? And beginning at Moses and all the prophets, he expounded unto them in all the scriptures the things concerning himself.

And they drew nigh unto the village, whither they went: and he made as though he would have gone further.

But they constrained him, saying, Abide with us: for it is toward evening, and the day is far spent. And he went in to tarry with them. And it came to pass, as he sat and ate with them, he

Chapter 18: Behold the Man

took bread, and blessed it, and brake, and gave to them.

And their eyes were opened, and they knew him; and he vanished out of their sight. And they said one to another; did not our heart burn within us, while he talked with us by the way, and while he opened to us the scriptures?

And they rose up the same hour, and returned to Jerusalem, and found the eleven gathered together, and them that were with them, Saying, The Lord is risen indeed, and hath appeared to Simon.

And they told what things were done in the way, and how he was known of them in breaking of bread. And as they thus spake, Jesus himself stood in the midst of them, and saith unto them, Peace be unto you.

But they were terrified and affrighted, and supposed that they had seen a spirit. And he said unto them, why are ye troubled? And why do thoughts arise in your hearts?

Behold my hands and my feet, that it is I myself: handle me, and see; for a spirit hath not flesh and bones, as ye see me have. And when he had thus spoken, he shewed them his hands and his feet.

And while they yet believed not for joy, and wondered, he said unto them, Have ye here any meat? And they gave him a piece of a broiled fish, and of honeycomb. And he took it, and did eat before them.

And he said unto them, These are the words which I spake unto you, while I was yet with you, that all things must be fulfilled, which were written in the law of Moses, and in the prophets, and in the psalms, concerning me.

Then opened he their understanding, that they might understand the scriptures, And said unto them, Thus it is written, and thus it behooved Christ to suffer, and to rise from the dead the third day: And that repentance and remission of sins should be preached in his name among all nations, beginning at Jerusalem. And ye are witnesses of these things.

And, behold, I send the promise of my Father upon you:

but tarry ye in the city of Jerusalem, until ye be endued with power from on high. And he led them out as far as to Bethany, and he lifted up his hands, and blessed them.

And it came to pass, while he blessed them, he was parted from them, and carried up into heaven. And they worshipped him, and returned to Jerusalem with great joy: And were continually in the temple, praising and blessing God. Amen."

What a man! With whom can we compare Him? The only problem for humanity is who would believe our report? How would the unaided mind accept the inalterable testimony of the holy God that God the Creator of the universe once walked on the streets of the earth for the purpose of saving His lost human creatures?

He cannot be just a man and neither is He just God. Jesus Christ is indeed the God-Man (fully God and fully man). Jesus Christ is the only door through which a man may enter to approach God. He is the only perfect sacrifice that can atone for man's sins and sin. He is the only priest who can plead and overturn the guilty verdict of failed humanity before the holy God.

Jesus is the only name by which man can be saved. God has given Him power over all flesh, that Jesus should give eternal life to as many as He would give Him (cf. John 17:2; cf. Acts 1:1-5; 1 John 1:1-4). There is life after death. Some men shall rise to enjoy eternal life with God and Christ, and others to everlasting condemnation in the Lake that burns with fire and sulfur:

> "Verily, verily, I say unto you, He that heareth my word, and believeth on him that sent me, hath everlasting life, and shall not come into condemnation; but is passed from death unto life" (John 5:24).

> "But the fearful, and unbelieving, and the abominable, and murderers, and whoremongers, and sorcerers, and idolaters, and all liars, shall have their part in the lake

Chapter 18: Behold the Man

which burneth with fire and brimstone: which is the second death" (Revelation 21:8).

But, for all those who receive Jesus Christ as Lord and Savior, nothing can separate them from the love of God. As the Scripture says, "Who shall separate us from the love of Christ? Shall tribulation, or distress, or persecution, or famine, or nakedness, or peril, or sword?" "For I am persuaded, that neither death, nor life, nor angels, nor principalities, nor powers, nor things present, nor things to come, nor height, nor depth, nor any other creature, shall be able to separate us from the love of God, which is in Christ Jesus our Lord" (Romans 8:35-39).

All who hate Jesus Christ love death (Proverbs 8:36). The Jehovah of the Old Testament is the Jesus Christ of the New Testament. By Him all things were created and consist and by Him all men can find salvation and rest for their souls. Jesus Christ is truly the Messiah-Savior-King.

Can you now appreciate why the title of this book is, "The Man Nobody Can Ignore?" There is no life outside Jesus Christ. He is the life and the light of this world. He died for you as well as for every other person born to this earth.

"Now unto him that is able to do exceeding abundantly above all that we ask or think, according to the power that worketh in us, unto him be glory in the church by Christ Jesus throughout all ages, world without end. Amen."

"May the Lord bless you, and keep you; the Lord make his face to shine upon you, and be gracious unto you" for reading this book. Amen.

Notes

THE EPITOME OF CHRISTIAN TRUTH

"And this is the record, that God hath given to us eternal life, and this life is in his Son. He that hath the Son hath life; and he that hath not the Son of God hath not life.

These things have I written unto you that believe on the name of the Son of God; that ye may know that ye have eternal life, and that ye may believe on the name of the Son of God" (1 John 5:11-13).

ABOUT THE AUTHOR

Joseph DeGraft-Amanfu is a disciple of Jesus Christ, a missionary, author and a Bible teacher. He is currently the President of Preach the Gospel 2 All, Inc., a ministry that focuses on soul-winning and discipleship.

He is a born again, Bible believer who accepts the inerrant inspiration of Scripture, fears the Lord and full of the Holy Spirit.

DeGraft-Amanfu attributes His entire Biblical learning and work to the Holy Spirit who has being his teacher and instructor for 36 years. He and his family currently reside in the United States of America.

He travels around the world teaching and preaching the Gospel of Jesus Christ. He also accepts teaching and preaching engagements from across the world.

For contact:
info@preachthegospel2all.com
www.preachthegospel2all.com

Breinigsville, PA USA
01 February 2010

231666BV00004B/2/P